Praise for The Killing Hour Series

BEFORE THE KILLING (Book One)

"Once I started I couldn't put it down!"
-Bookshelf Adventures

"Mystery fans will love this plot device, which takes a straightforward whodunit to an otherworldly level."
-The BookLife Prize

"A cleverly plotted fantasy thriller with a strong cast of characters."
-The Wishing Shelf Book Awards

BEFORE SHE WAS TAKEN (Book Two)

"This was such an amazing novel to read... The characters were wonderfully written and very easy to like. I found myself unable to put it down... This novel was a fast read for me and I greatly recommend it. I can't wait to continue with the series in the future." -Bookshelf Adventures

"The plot moves at an even pace and has a surprising ending; this supernatural mystery will be enjoyed by a diverse array of readers... the book has a strong female character who is easy to follow, smart, and displays agency."
-The BookLife Prize

BEFORE HE VANISHED

The Killing Hour Book Three

MARGIE BENEDICT

FIRST EDITION, MARCH 2022

Publisher: margiebenedict.com
Cover Design: GetCovers.com

ISBN: 978-1-954584-29-7 (paperback)

Printed in the United States of America

For Tanner, Alan, and Derek

Rebecca

Chapter One

REBECCA HAD THOUGHT her sister's safe return would end her obsession with child abduction cases, yet somehow her walk has led her to the same *Missing Person* poster for the second day in a row.

The first time she had the excuse that sidewalk construction blocked her normal route. But today she actually chose this direction, although it brought her to a dark and dreary section of town. The buildings on either side of the street are stark and far-reaching, marked by splotches of mud and graffiti at their lower levels. Trash spills out from alleyways, suspicious-looking characters lurk in doorways, and the stench of urine overpowers every other smell.

As before, she has paused at the flyer tacked onto the utility pole near the X-rated bookstore. It looks like someone produced it using their crappy inkjet printer at home. The black ink is faded, and the white spaces are grimy. At the bottom, the paper has been cut into matching strips with the phone number printed on them. It's an old-fashioned thing to do in the age of the cell phone. But maybe it's only her place of privilege that makes it difficult for her to imagine someone tearing off a slip of paper instead of saving the number on their cell with a photo.

A thirteen-year-old child is pictured on the notice. Rebecca knows his age because it says so at the bottom. He has coffee-colored skin, rosebud lips, and charcoal hair cut close to his scalp. No smile. He looks impatient. Is it because he really doesn't want his picture to be taken? Or he's anxious to be somewhere? Or he's weary of a world that's become all too much for him?

The text underneath the photo says, "MISSING. Ethan Pitt. Last seen on…" a date that's roughly a year ago. The text includes the name of the city where he lives, and an exhortation to call the number "if you have any information regarding his whereabouts."

She doesn't call the number, but does Google his name and the date he vanished. One small news item turns up, reporting his disappearance several days after it happened. That's all. There is no further mention of him on the Internet. No way to know if he simply ran away and later returned home, or if he's still missing, or if his body has been found and whether his death was ruled an accident, suicide, or murder.

Simply no information at all.

Her thoughts fly to her sister Sadie. It was a huge story when she was kidnapped. She was an adorable little white girl. Though they failed, law enforcement put a great deal of effort into searching for her. Local police and the FBI vied for control of the investigation. News services swarmed their family and friends. Until they didn't.

Who cries for Ethan Pitt? she wonders.

Ethan

Chapter Two

ETHAN SLOUCHES in front of the classroom, his hands trembling as he clutches the paper. "Amari is gathering wood for the fire when he hears the first scream coming from the village. Soon the air is filled with the cries of women and the shouts of men. Though the sound terrifies him, Amari runs fleet-footed back to the king tree and peeks out from behind it to find out what has happened.

"The invaders have pink skin, pinched features, and thick clothing that covers every part of them except their faces and hands. They have surrounded the villagers, including Amari's own parents and older sister. When Chikere—a young man who carves wood into animal shapes—tries to escape, one of the invaders snaps a rope at him. It cuts into his back and causes him to bleed. His anguished cry pierces Amari through the heart.

"The invaders bind the villagers one to another using a chain made of a hard, inflexible material like stone, not like the grasses his mother weaves into rope. They work quickly, before the villagers can figure out how to resist them. The invaders are, in fact, smaller and weaker than the men of Amari's village, but there are more of them, and they have used the advantage of surprise to good effect.

"Amari watches, frozen in fear and indecision. What can he, a thirteen-year-old boy, do to save his loved ones? He remains in hiding while everyone he knows in the world is shepherded away by the invaders.

"During the night, he curls up into a ball and weeps. But in the morning, the sunrise brings him new courage. He takes the spear that belongs to his father and a small supply of food and water before setting out to track the invaders and save his village."

Ethan lowers the paper and glances at Mr. Flannery, hoping to be allowed to sit down. But his teacher is slumped at his desk, looking oddly shrunken in his jacket that seems too large for him, and his neck extending forward like a turtle's. He peers at his students through his oversized black-rimmed glasses with the same expression he always wears—like he's resigned to bearing the burden of the world upon his shoulders.

"Pink skin?" Malcolm asks. No one ever waits to be called on in this class. It takes much worse infractions to trigger their teacher's temper. The cold venom that emerges during those rare moments is a terrible thing to witness, however.

"They have sunburns," Ethan says. "You know? White guys in Africa? They're gonna have sunburns."

Mr. Flannery, whose fungus green sweater contrasts with his own pasty hue, makes no comment.

"Why'd you say the women cry and the men shout?" Yolanda asks. "Seems really gender-biased."

Ethan was expecting this. He saw her scribbling a note to

herself when he said that. Yolanda's comments are always about gender bias. "Yeah, I guess," he says. "I'll change it." It's easier not to argue with her, and anyway, he doesn't care about the kids in the back who snicker.

"What's a king tree?" This from the new student. Ethan doesn't remember his name.

"It's just what they call it. The biggest tree around, you know?"

"Ethan, you can sit." Though he enunciates every word, Mr. Flannery's sentences have a way of sounding flat. "Class, after hearing this first chapter, who wants to read more?"

Several hands shoot up while others give an unenthusiastic wave. The troublemakers in the back raise bored eyes to the clock.

Ethan drops into his front-row seat with relief. He wasn't happy when his teacher picked him to read his homework aloud, particularly since he didn't come up with the story idea himself. It begins like many told to him by his uncle over the years. Still, Ethan added his own details and came up with the wording. Uncle Ray never gave him written copies of his stories, though he had binders full of his handwritten scrawl. According to his uncle, Ethan has a way with language and he's miles ahead of other kids his age in writing skills. His problem is a lack of original ideas. When he started the assignment, he stared for hours at the blank page before deciding there wouldn't be any harm in borrowing from Uncle Ray.

Mr. Flannery zeroes in on Teshi, who's bent over her desk doodling on a piece of paper. "Why didn't you raise your hand when I asked who wanted to read more of Ethan's story?"

Ethan is thinking, *Why'd he have to ask her?*

"I do wanna read it." Teshi says.

"Okay then. Why?"

"Cuz Ethan wrote it. Gotta be good. Learned that shit from his uncle." Teshi flashes Ethan a knowing smile. The two of them hung together a lot in elementary school, and Teshi has listened to plenty of Uncle Ray's stories.

Mr. Flannery tolerates swearing unless someone goes on a rant. "You mean you trust Ethan to tell a good story?"

"Like I said. Got it from his uncle." Teshi seems one slip of the tongue away from accusing Ethan of plagiarism.

"How else does Ethan hook us into his story?" Mr. Flannery's gaze flicks across the room.

The bell rings, putting an instant end to any discussion. Chairs scrape as students leap up, forcing Mr. Flannery to raise his voice. "Work on your next chapters. I'll be picking someone else to read next time."

No one is listening anymore as they jostle to be first to the door. When Ethan reaches the hallway, Teshi catches up to him. "Weird," she says. "The pink faces, the king tree… feel like I heard that shit before."

He twists the dark brown and blue braided leather wristband his father gave him and tries to move past her. But there's a scent surrounding her, something delightful like peaches and honey, that makes him pause and look up. For the first time, it hits him how pretty she is. She used to be a scrawny little thing, and now she's taller than him. Though she's still thin, curves are forming in all the right places. Her smile radiates warmth and light and makes him helpless to do anything but smile back.

"Did you see these?" She nods down at her feet.

"Who'd you have to rob to pay for those fire Air Jordans?" he says. Teshi's family is dirt poor and probably ten bucks away from homeless. Maybe that wasn't nice of him to say, but he hasn't gotten over being annoyed with her.

His jab doesn't faze her, though. "What you gonna pay me to find out?" She parades her feet down the corridor, in no hurry to get to her next class.

Chapter Three

AFTER SCHOOL, Ethan plans to visit Uncle Ray to get ideas for the rest of his story. But when he reaches into his pocket, he discovers he left his money at home.

He considers heading back, but One Fine Burger, the fast-food joint where his mother works, is closer. And if he goes there, she'll get him something to eat too.

When he arrives, Ma is preparing food in the back, but as usual, she senses his arrival and looks over just as he's approaching. Her face brightens like it always does when she sees him.

He waits off to the side until she has a second to join him. "You want a burger?" she says. Off his nod, she teases, "Course you do."

"Ma, I need three bucks. I owe it to Lamar." He's a sixteen-year-old kid who lives in their building. Ma likes him because he's a geek who works hard in school.

"You shouldn't borrow money."

"Sorry." He feels guilty for lying. When he visits Uncle

Ray, he always slips him a few bucks. If Ma knew it was for him, she wouldn't give Ethan a penny.

Cecelia, who always has a sour face, finishes with a customer before Ma squeezes past her to the register and pays for Ethan's order. "Catch more flies with honey," Ma says to her. "Time to time, you might try smiling."

Cecilia scowls worse. "They gonna buy their burgers no matter what."

Ma returns to her work in the back and a few minutes later she hands over a medium Coke along with a bag that Ethan knows will contain a cheeseburger even though she ordered him a plain, a large-sized portion of fries though she ordered small, and four packets of ketchup. When he opens it, he finds the three dollars in there too.

Ethan polishes off the food in no time at all at a table outside. He sets off on his board and reaches the tent city under the freeway within twenty minutes. The place looks like an even worse shithole than the last time he came, and he has to cover his nose because it reeks like a garbage dump. He picks his way carefully, anxious to avoid stepping on syringes or piles of shit. A rat skitters from underneath one discarded food wrapper to another. It breaks Ethan's heart that his uncle has nowhere better to live.

He spots Uncle Ray looking worked up about something as he speaks to a man wearing a hat from the last century and a ragged, threadbare suit. Noticing Ethan's approach, Ray turns away from the man and hurries toward his nephew. He looks distraught, as close to tears as Ethan has ever seen him.

"What's happening?" Ethan says.

"It's gone." He shakes his head miserably. "It's all gone."

"What do you mean?"

He lowers his voice. "All my cash. Everything I saved up."

Ethan glances around and moves in closer so as not to be overheard. "You told me you always carry it on you."

Uncle Ray nods. "They picked my pockets while I was sleeping."

"You didn't wake up?"

Uncle Ray throws up his hands. "Sometimes I take a little something to help me sleep. Else how am I going to get any rest in this place?"

"Yeah, I get it." Ethan glances toward his uncle's tent. "Did you look everywhere? Maybe it fell out of your pocket."

"First thing I thought was I lost it. Tore through all my shit looking for it. It's gone, Ethan. I got nothing." His shoulders sag. "What am I going to do?"

If Uncle Ray was a person of means, who lived in a real home, who had connections in his community, maybe he could go to the police. Maybe they would actually make some effort to find the thief. But as it was, the police would laugh him out of the station if he went there to report the theft. There was no recourse for people like Uncle Ray.

Ethan takes out the dollar bills Ma gave him and presses it into his uncle's hands. "At least you can eat something." *Just barely.*

"Boy, I can't take your money." Uncle Ray always says this before taking the money.

"I'll try to bring more tomorrow." It won't be easy. Ma won't help Uncle Ray even if Ethan tells her what happened. She blames him for the drug deal that went bad and landed him and Ethan's dad behind bars. She blames him worse for his father having gotten sick and died in there, while Uncle Ray eventually made it out of prison alive.

"What about that job interview you had?" Ethan says.

He blows out air. "Train I was on just sat on the track for

an hour. Nobody ever did explain that. So I didn't get there till late, and then the man just told me to leave, didn't want to hire anyone who couldn't get there on time. I was saving for a car, you know? It's all I need. I can live in it. I can get places, if I have a car. I was thinking of driving to San Diego. People tell me it's nicer there. I should've gone already, on the bus. Then I'd still have my money. Now I got to start from square one. Don't know how I'm going to do it. Nobody gives you the time of day when you got a record."

Ethan only wishes he could help. He's sorry he came here for the selfish reason of wanting Uncle Ray to give him more story ideas. Of all the stupid things, compared to the hell his uncle goes through every day of his life. It isn't fair. It wasn't his fault his money was stolen, dashing all his hopes to better himself and escape this pit of despair.

Chapter Four

WHEN ETHAN OPENS the door to their apartment, he's surprised not to smell anything cooking. Usually by this time his mother has made soup, or beans, or mac and cheese, or any of the other frugal meals they typically eat. Before he turned thirteen, the burger after school might've held him till morning, but these days he's got a gnawing hunger that needs satisfying every few hours.

A glance into the kitchen confirms nothing is on the stove and the breakfast dishes are still soaking in the sink. Not a good sign. Ma doesn't start on the meal until the dishes are washed and put away.

He's thinking she must be out, maybe doing some shopping, but then he sees her in the family room, seated in the corner chair. She's not looking at him, doesn't even seem aware that he's there. Her eyes are glazed over, staring into space at nothing. This isn't like her. Normally she has the TV on, or if not that, she's reading an ebook on her phone. She downloads free romance novels wherever she can find them online.

"Hey Ma," he says. "Did you eat?"

She blinks and looks at him blankly, like she has to think about it. "I guess not." She doesn't move to get up, though.

"Everything okay?"

"Of course it's okay." Her tone is sharp. "Why wouldn't it be?"

He opens the fridge and the cupboards to see what their options are. "I can make us hot dogs," he says.

"I'm not hungry. Just make it for yourself."

"You sure?"

When she doesn't answer, he cooks two. If she won't eat the extra one, he will.

"Where were you?" she says, suddenly sounding more alert.

"Hanging with my bros." He doesn't want to tell her about his visit to Uncle Ray when she's already in a bad mood. "Don't worry, I did my homework, except English." He'll have to come up with something to move the story forward since he didn't get the help he was hoping for from his uncle.

"I saw Lamar in the hall. He told me you never owed him any money," Ma says.

"Thought I did."

"Well, you didn't. So let me have that cash back. We could use it."

His brain scrambles to think of a way out of this. He pats his pants like he thinks the money's still there. "Must've fallen out of my pocket."

She gives him the stink eye. "Don't you lie to me. You gave it to that no-good uncle of yours, didn't you?" It's not a question.

He's silent, knowing there's no point in lying because she can always tell just by looking at him.

"I told you not to go there," she says.

"He's my uncle."

"He broke the law. And he lives in that tent city full of addicts and rapists and who knows what all else."

"He's got nowhere else to live. You know how hard it is for him to get a job with his record? What's up with that? You serve your time, you should get another chance."

"He's a bad influence. You stay away from him." She is particularly ornery this evening, and he wishes he knew why.

"He needs help, Ma. Somebody found his money stash and stole it."

"That's what happens when you live with all the lowlifes."

He's never seen her this unsympathetic before.

"We can't help him. We're just barely getting by. You'll have to start working, Ethan."

He looks up in surprise. "You told me not to. School comes first, you always said."

"You were younger then. At thirteen, there's stuff you can do."

"Stuff like what?"

"I don't know. Deliver papers? Mow lawns?"

"I can't drive! And who's got a lawn big enough to mow around here?"

"Well, you figure it out. Ask your friends. Time you pulled your own weight." She jabs the TV remote and turns the volume high, making it clear she doesn't want to hear another word from him.

He sits at the table with his meal, but the lump in his throat makes swallowing hard.

Chapter Five

AS SOON AS HE WAKES, Ethan looks over the chapter he wrote the night before. The visit to his uncle proved useful after all. The theft that happened while Uncle Ray slept, and Ma's talk of rapists at the camp gave Ethan the ideas he needed.

He's surprised to find the kitchen empty. His mother doesn't normally sleep this long. Although her shift doesn't start till later, she likes to help him with breakfast and see him off on the bus.

He toasts two pieces of bread and spreads peanut butter on them. There's precious little else in the cupboards. When he's done eating, he'll have to wake Ma up and let her know. Hopefully she'll do the shopping before heading to work.

He didn't get much rest last night. First, he stayed up too late writing his story. Then he slept fitfully through a series of dreams he can't remember now. It's probably because he's worried about Uncle Ray, and Ma too. Something was bothering her and it was strange she didn't tell him about it, because normally she talks his ear off when the slightest thing goes wrong.

Something must have happened at the job. Her supervisor yelled at her, or a customer talked smack to her. She tries to take things in stride, but she's sensitive and sometimes the shit people say gets under her skin. Ethan understands. He's the same way whenever one of his teachers raises his voice at him, or accuses him of something he didn't do. Like that time Mr. Howard thought he stole supplies from the classroom. It was so unfair and untrue. Luckily his last year homeroom teacher stuck up for him and put Mr. Howard in his place.

He pours himself the last bit of orange juice and puts his dishes in the sink. If he misses the bus, he'll have to use his board and then he'll get detention for being late to his first period class. After tossing his homework into his backpack, he checks on his mother. She's seated in bed, filling her glass from a bottle of vodka.

"Ma?"

She looks up, bleary-eyed.

"Why're you starting so early on that stuff?" It's happened before, like when his father was arrested and all the shit after that. But he hasn't seen her do it in a while.

"Don't you go judging your momma. Just for today, I need a little something to make me feel better."

"What're you feeling so bad about?"

"What are you doing here still? You're going to be late for school."

"We need groceries today."

"You pick them up after school."

"I need guap for that."

"Check my wallet."

He opens her purse on top of the dresser. "There's only eight bucks here."

She shrugs. "Get what you can."

DURING LUNCH BREAK, Ethan slips away from school to check on his mother at work and see if she's gotten into a better mood. He prays she didn't drink too much, because that's how she got fired from her last job.

When he gets there, he doesn't see her behind the counter or in the back. He waits, thinking she's using the bathroom. But five minutes later, when she still hasn't come out, he approaches the heavy woman with spikey hair who's been nice to him before.

"Have you seen my Ma?" he says.

The woman scrunches up her face. "No, honey, not today."

"But she always works on Tuesdays." He wonders if she called in sick.

"Yeah, well, you better ask her about that."

Her tone conveys the worst. "Did she get fired?" he whispers.

The woman glances behind her nervously. "Like I said, you need to talk to her about that." She moves away to assist a customer.

That's it then, he thinks. She got fired. No wonder she wanted him to look for a job. Jesus. Thirteen years old, and now he's got to support Ma and Uncle Ray both.

Rebecca

Chapter Six

REBECCA BANGS the plate of Indian takeout leftovers on the kitchen table and drops into her seat. It grates that neither her sister nor anyone else will be warming the empty place across from her for she-doesn't-know-how-long.

Covid-19 did this. Beginning last month, the potentially deadly virus sent Americans scurrying back inside their homes, but only after they emptied supermarket shelves of hand sanitizer, toilet paper, and yeast. Why people seemed to require five-year supplies of the first two items is beyond her, but the run on yeast is even more baffling. Suddenly everyone is making their own bread, as if bakeries are the one mode of food production poised to disappear off the face of the earth. *C'mon, people. We're not homesteading here.*

She opens her laptop on the table to start the Zoom with Sadie. They used to have lunch dates in person, but now everyone has been ordered not to mingle indoors with anyone outside their own household. Those with a household of one can kiss human contact goodbye for the foreseeable future.

Sadie's face on the screen cheers her instantly, though. It's still surreal to have her little sister back in her life. "What're you eating?" she says.

"Chicken tikka masala. You?"

Sadie lifts a grilled cheese sandwich into the camera view.

"Again?" Rebecca says.

"Don't judge me."

"How's the fam?"

"Gone hiking at Tilden Park." Sadie takes a bite and keeps talking. "Becca, I wish you would join us here. You must be lonely."

She had moved out of Rebecca's apartment and into their father's home in Berkeley before the pandemic began. Martin had been visiting a lot then, and despite Rebecca's reassurances, Sadie had become convinced her presence got in the way of their romance.

"I'm fine," Rebecca says in a sharper tone than she meant.

"What about Martin? Is that really over?"

"He can't get himself to move away from Draywood. I mean, he's been there all his life. And I can't live there." She doesn't say she couldn't bear to occupy the same town where Sadie was kept prisoner for most of her life up till now. But her sister understands. "We might've been able to do a long-distance relationship if it wasn't for this damn virus. Anyway, it's over."

"Do you want me to move back in with you?"

"I'm fine. Really. You should stay with Dad."

Sadie sips her sparkling water before looking up again. "I do like being here."

"I know you do." It stings to see how close she and their

father have become in such a short time. She even gets on well with his wife. Rebecca has always thought Marie couldn't stand her. How else to explain that they never asked *her* to live with them?

"It's not just him," Sadie goes on. "I can't get enough of our little brothers. It's just… amazing being part of a real family instead of one built on lies and intimidation."

What a gentle soul my sister is. Rebecca would've used a much harsher expression than "lies and intimidation." *Unfathomable cruelty*, more like.

"Little sis, you deserve to be as happy as you possibly can. I won't allow you to change anything. I'm absolutely fine."

"Tell me what you're doing these days," Sadie says.

With the pandemic going on, Rebecca's classes are in flux, neither in-person nor electronic at the moment. They're supposed to transition to online in a month. But she's already lost interest in them. She had started studying math and computer science at their father's urging. For years, he'd insisted she ought to develop the skills that would help her build a career. For years she'd resisted, until Sadie returned and it seemed as if she could finally have a normal life. But her life still does not feel normal. *She* does not feel normal.

"I'm keeping busy enough." She isn't, though. Her days consist of long walks with her face covered in a mask, getting takeout food for her meals, doing math puzzles, reading books, watching Netflix. *I hate my life*, is the thought that flashes weirdly across her brain. But she isn't about to tell Sadie. "What about you?"

"Still full steam ahead with pre-med. I'm lucky there's plenty I can do from home."

"Make us proud."

But Sadie is not done picking apart her sister. "I worry about you."

This makes Rebecca smile. Sadie, whose childhood was stolen… worried about *her*.

"Any time you need me, just let me know and I'll be there in a flash," Sadie says.

"It goes both ways."

"You've done your part. You nearly got yourself killed for me."

"I hadn't planned on that."

"I need to ask you something. I hope it won't upset you," Sadie says. "Dad doesn't like to talk about it, so I thought…"

Rebecca, chewing, nods for her to continue.

"It's about Mom." Her voice lowers. "That's been the hardest thing to accept since I got back. That she lost hope. That she gave up on finding me."

Imagine if you were the daughter who didn't go missing, Rebecca thinks. *Imagine if you were a needy eight-year-old living with said mother, but she didn't see you as sufficient reason to cling to life.* Rebecca says nothing, though. She doesn't want to burden Sadie with her pain.

"I wish I could've gotten to know her as an adult," Sadie says. "I remember nothing about her except a vague feeling of warmth and love. I know she was a writer. Do you have anything she wrote that I can read?"

Another sore point for Rebecca. "She finished a novel, then destroyed every copy before she died. Of all the things… I really can't forgive her for that."

"Did she leave a letter? Or a note?"

Rebecca's skin tingles. "A note?"

"You know… a suicide note. Something that could give

some insight into her thoughts. I don't know. I was just wondering."

"There was no letter. No note. I'm sorry." But just as the words leave Rebecca's mouth, an image flashes inside her head. Her mother's body on the bed, and beside her on the table, a piece of paper.

Chapter Seven

IN THE EVENING, Rebecca fails to focus on the math problems she promised herself she would work on while her classes are in flux. All she can think about is how her mother might've left a suicide note she was never allowed to read. A debate rages inside her head over whether that piece of paper is a figment of her imagination, or whether it's a dormant memory that shot to the surface at Sadie's suggestion.

If there had been any such thing, her father ought to have told her by now. Maybe he didn't want her to see it when she was a child, but there was no excuse for not sharing it with her as soon as she reached adulthood. *Or was there?* If the note said something awful like *fuck you*, her father might be forgiven for simply destroying it. What good could come of sharing such bitterness with a child? She wouldn't want to show it to her kid either, if she had one.

Or maybe the note was just pointless. Something that revealed nothing about her mother. *Farewell*, or *I couldn't take it anymore*, or *yes, this really is a suicide*.

Eventually, she gives up on doing any work and tries to

watch a streaming show. When it too fails to gain her attention, she shuts off her TV and prepares for bed.

Lying on her back in the darkness, she wonders if she still might have the power to travel through time. She thought she had lost it after Sadie was found, because the ability seemed to be driven by her needs and sense of purpose. But since then, she'd only tried once, and when the attempt failed, she thought that might be the end of it.

Now she wonders if it didn't work because she had nothing motivating her on that occasion. Since she became a time traveler, her mindcasts have always been driven by strong emotional need. Even the ones involving meaningless sex with Dev probably arose from wanting to fill the emptiness inside her.

It started the day she'd been hiking by herself and briefly wandered off trail. A tiny flash of light seemed to jump out of a black rock and prick her skin. It had caused a tingling sensation and nothing more. She paid so little attention to it, she continued on her walk and never thought there might be a reason to save that special rock. Now she would never find it again.

She still isn't one hundred percent certain her time traveling ability came from the rock, but since it was the only unusual thing that happened shortly before she discovered her new power, she has come to accept it as the explanation. Maybe aliens scattered them, thinking it would be funny to give humans a new power they had no clue how to use.

The first time she did a mindcast, as she later decided to call it, it was the strangest feeling. First her vision went black, then the inside of her head became hotter than her face the time she went to Florida and burned so bad she looked like a boiled lobster. As the heat lessened, dizziness overcame her, along with the sensation of doing reverse somersaults. *Like falling backward through time.* It was always backward, never forward.

Since her initial mindcasts brought her only to the recent past, it took several iterations before she was certain that only her thoughts had jumped back. In other words, when she traveled into the past there were not two Rebeccas wandering around. *Youth is wasted on the young*, they say. Here was a way for an older mind to experience youth again.

She eventually learned the other key aspect of her mindcasts—she could not change history. No matter what she did, when she returned to real-time, nothing in her life, or in the world, was changed. Maybe her mindcasts sent her into a parallel time thread, but she soon gave up thinking about it, since it only made her head hurt. Time travel allowed her to witness the past and to play with alternate scenarios that would never go anywhere in her own real-time. It had been all she needed to locate Sadie.

Tonight, for the first time since her sister came home, Rebecca has a powerful desire to revisit a moment in her past. She concentrates on that day, visualizing everything she can recall about it. And before long, a match is lit inside her head and she is spinning backward.

Chapter Eight

2002 - MINDCAST

REBECCA IS eight years old and dreading what she and her father are going to discover inside her mother's house, although she knows what it is.

She's standing outside the front door next to Dad, staring up at his profile and wondering how she could have forgotten how handsome he'd been at this age. His clean-shaven face reveals the chiseled jaw that will later be covered by heavy bristle. He has smooth, dusty red hair that will, eighteen years from now, be reduced to thin gray strands across an otherwise bald head.

As he rings the doorbell for the second time, she looks down at herself and tries to wrap her brain around her much smaller, weaker self. She has mindcast into her little girl body twice before, but it's just as freaky the third time around. Because it's summer, she's wearing a tank top, shorts, and sandals. Her knobby little knees poke out below the shorts, but the real highlight is the pink glitter polish she must've spent hours applying to her miniature toenails.

"Did she say anything to you?" her father says, not really expecting an answer.

"No, Daddy." Her squeaky little-girl voice startles her.

He's annoyed because he has plans for tonight and wanted to get back quickly. But then he tries the knob, as Rebecca knows he will, and raises his eyebrows on finding it open. When she follows him in, she's overwhelmed by how surreal it feels, seeing her home the way it was all those years ago. She'll never grow accustomed to jumping this far into her past. It will always seem more like a dream than real life.

When he glances back to check on her, she notices the moisture beading on his forehead. It's like an oven in this place. They had central air conditioning added months before Sadie was taken, but it clearly isn't running now.

The rooms are far neater than she recalls. Everything in its place. The scent of lavender potpourri clings to the hot, suffocating atmosphere. Though it seems like someone contemplating suicide must have weightier matters to consider, her mother has shown a strange consideration in the details. *You won't have to clean up after me*, she hears her mother say. *You won't have to pay for air conditioning no one was using.*

"Take my hand, Rebecca," her dad says. Although his palms are sticky, she does so gladly. He knows something is wrong, but isn't sure if that wrong thing might involve a home invader. His instincts morph into protect-the-child mode.

They take a quick survey of the downstairs rooms, finding them empty. At the bottom of the stairs, they listen for movement. But the house is silent except for the ticking of the wall clock in the family room. Before, she would've taken that as a reminder of time's unstoppable forward motion, but lately she's been picturing it as more of a circular thing.

"Camille?" her dad calls out, not too loudly.

"Mommy," Rebecca says, she's not sure why, since she knows there will be no answer.

He calls her mother's name again. When no reply comes, he grips Rebecca's hand tighter and starts up the steps. He fears what they'll find upstairs, but the thought of leaving his child alone in this house frightens him more. He hasn't fully ruled out the possibility of an intruder yet.

She stumbles on a step, betrayed by her short, spindly legs. He lifts her up. This is a new detail. The genuine eight-year-old Rebecca would not have tripped over her own feet.

They reach her mother's bedroom door, which Rebecca remembers was left ajar. He lowers her, keeping her away from the opening, blocking her view of the room with his body. Only then does he turn and peer in. Rebecca knows he sees his former wife lying on the bed with her face turned away from them.

"Camille?" he says softly.

The same dread Rebecca feels inside her small torso is evident in her father's voice. This is so much harder than she thought it would be. To arrive here, at this moment, when it's too late to save her. If only they had come earlier… if only they had understood her state of mind… if only someone could've helped her and prevented her from taking this final act. It hurts even more knowing that if her mother had remained alive, she and Sadie would've been reunited. The rest of her life could've been filled with joy.

Her father moves around the bed and kneels beside her mother. Rebecca sees it now, a piece of paper on the bedside table. She runs toward it, but before she can reach it, he sweeps her up into his arms.

"Lemme go!" she cries in her childish voice.

Tears course down his cheeks as he holds her to him and carries her from the room. "You need to wait out here." He sets her down in the hall and returns to the bedroom, shutting and locking the door after him.

She bangs on the door with her round little fists. "Let me in! I want to see her!"

She hears him place a phone call to emergency services. Soon after, he opens the door again. "All right, Rebecca. Mommy is gone. You understand?"

She nods her head, sniffing.

"You can see her now. You can say goodbye to her."

At the time, she probably asked if Mommy was ever coming back, or how did it happen that her Mommy is now dead? But she says none of that now. When he lets her into the room, she dashes toward the other side of the bed, only to have her hopes crushed.

The piece of paper is gone.

"She left a note," Rebecca says. "Where is it?"

Her father gives her a curious look, surprised that she even noticed. "There wasn't any note," he says.

"You're lying! There was! Let me see it!" She grabs at his pocket.

He carries her kicking and screaming to the hallway and shuts the door on her again. As the lock clicks inside the room, her mindcast ends.

Chapter Nine

THREE MORE TIMES over the following week, Rebecca travels back to the day she and her father found her mother. She tries to outwit him by dashing up the stairs ahead of him, or slipping around his legs into the bedroom, but he blocks her every attempt to get her pudgy hands on the note. Eight-year-old Rebecca can't get past her father when he's determined to prevent it.

The situation infuriates her. How dare he keep her from reading her mother's last words? Why, after all these years, has he never mentioned it? Even if he thought she couldn't handle it as a child, he should have given it to her when she turned eighteen. But he's never said a single damn thing about it.

She considers telling him that a repressed memory regarding the note has emerged, and would he please show it to her? But if he's truly determined to keep her from reading it, he might deny its existence and then destroy it, if he hasn't already. She decides not to say anything unless the right moment somehow presents itself.

As for mindcasting back to that horrible day, she is done, at least for now. Each time they rediscover her dead mother's body is like another twist of the knife through her heart. She needs a rest from it.

REBECCA WALKS the Filbert Street Steps as often as she can. This is one of the great benefits of San Francisco compared to where she used to live in the 'burbs, and the main reason she hesitates to leave the city, despite that rent would be cheaper almost anywhere else. The stairs are a challenging workout and on a clear day, she can view the broad expanse of the bay in exquisite detail. Other attractions include the quaint homes without parking spaces, the gardens with their flame-colored flowers, and best of all, the wild parrots.

Today, as sometimes happens, she questions her current life choices. She's known, almost since she started taking classes at community college, that she's really not interested in a career as a mathematician or a computer scientist or any other type of engineer. Only a reluctance to disappoint her father has kept her from quitting so far.

Why should she care? He didn't bother to consider how it might affect his daughter to hide her mother's last words from her forever.

Admittedly, she has no idea what she'll do if she drops the classes. No clue, really, regarding where to find contentment. She's been unhappy for years, but until recently, she thought it was because of Sadie being kidnapped. Now that they have her back, she wonders why her life hasn't been transformed.

Every second she spends in her sister's company brings her joy. It's the rest of the time that's the problem. There has to be more to living.

She slows her pace slightly to catch her breath on the uphill. Should she forget about a career and simply rely on her trust fund? That sounds boring, and besides, she doesn't expect it to last her whole life. She considers what skills she might have. Good at math, but uninterested in using that talent. Reliable, for the most part. Well-organized? Maybe not. Smart? Hard to judge.

Courage, though. She believes she has that. Not everyone could do what she did to save her sister. Courage and determination. When she decides to do something, she sticks with it.

She pauses to gaze at the Bay Bridge, its brilliant white lines etched into the deep blue sky. Her next thought makes her laugh. How could she have forgotten her one completely unique skill?

Visions of time travel lead her steps downward and onto a street she has visited twice before in recent days.

When she reaches the intersection where she believes the *Missing Person* flyer of Ethan Pitt was posted, she wonders if she made a mistake. The flyer is gone, though there are bits of paper hanging from tacks. Glancing around, she reassures herself that this was the spot. A thread of hope tickles her. Maybe Ethan's picture was removed because they found him.

Her hope is immediately dashed when she notices a crumpled wad of paper caught in the prickly branches of a dead shrub a few feet away. She snatches it and smooths open the page to find Ethan staring up at her with the N-word slashed in red ink across his face.

A wave of nausea hits her and she has to steady herself against the pole. The defilement of the flyer feels like a metaphor for Ethan's tragic life. Torn and sullied, abandoned and forgotten on this dismal, godforsaken street.

When she gets home, Rebecca opens her laptop and starts a new search for any mention of the boy. This time she finds him on a site called missingkids.org. The listing shows the same photo that was on the flyer, the date he went missing and from where, his race (black), his hair (black), his eye color (brown), his height (5'3"), and his weight (98 pounds).

The thought that he might not have lived long enough to push his weight into three digits makes her eyes well up.

Eventually she finds him on Facebook as well, sandwiched by a bra ad above and a cat meme below. Again, the identical photo, but different text. *Don't look away*, it says. *He could be your son, your grandchild, your brother. A thirteen-year-old child who disappeared. Don't you care? Doesn't anybody care? His name is Ethan Pitt. I'm his aunt. PM me if you know anything.*

That's all. Then beneath it, a name, *Yakeera McDade*, and the date of his disappearance.

Rebecca's cursor hovers over his picture for a long time before she clicks on his aunt's name. She writes, *Call me at...* and leaves her phone number. Let Yakeera make the first move, if *she* still cares.

Chapter Ten

2020 - PRESENT

REBECCA'S PHONE rings a few hours after she reaches out to Ethan's aunt. She thought the woman might call sooner, but when this much time has gone by and you're not expecting anyone to care, you're probably not checking your Facebook messages every second.

"This is Ethan's aunt. Yakeera McDade. Is this Rebecca?" She sounds impatient.

"Yes, that's me."

"What's your interest in Ethan?"

"I'd like to ask you some questions about his disappearance."

"Lady, I thought you had information for *me*."

Rebecca hadn't actually said that, but there's no point in arguing. "I'm sorry. No. That's not the reason for my call."

"Look, I Googled you. You had a missing sister you found recently, right?"

"That's right. Sadie."

"So, are you just obsessed with missing kids now? Calling up victim's families to compare notes? I don't get it."

"It's not like that. I do care about missing people because I've experienced the anguish of it firsthand. That's what drew me to Ethan's case. I'm a freelance writer. If I can gather enough information, I'd like to write an article about him."

"Freelance? You mean no one's paying you for this?"

"I hope to sell it to a newspaper or magazine."

"Why on earth do you think any paper would give good money for an article about Ethan?"

"Because people are finally talking about the fact that when something happens to a person of color, nobody in the white world is paying attention. The police don't put in much effort, the media barely mentions it. I want to change that."

"And we should trust you, a white woman, to tell our boy's story? Please."

"Is anyone else offering? You need publicity. People need to learn about him and be on the lookout for him. If the Chronicle publishes this, it'll put pressure on the police to do more. I'm going to do my best. Why not let me try?" Rebecca feels guilty lying to Yakeera, but she plans to make it up to her. If given the chance, she'll do her damnedest to find the boy.

"What do you want to know?" Yakeera finally says. "I've got nothing better to do right now."

A nervous shiver runs through Rebecca. Now that she's got the go-ahead, she almost wishes Ethan's aunt had called her bluff. If she had, Rebecca would've been saved from starting something that could be way beyond the scope of her meager abilities. Something that might be even more frightening and life-threatening than what she went through to save Sadie.

"Where was Ethan the last time anyone saw him?" Rebecca begins.

Ethan

Chapter Eleven

JUST AS ETHAN is leaving the locker room, his teacher calls his name. He freezes, certain he's about to get in trouble for being a total fuck-up on the basketball court today. Ever since lunch, he hasn't been able to think about anything aside from Ma losing her job and drinking again.

When he turns back, Mr. Johnson takes in his scared face and says, "Ethan, it's okay. I wanted to talk to you about something. You're not in trouble."

Ethan relaxes a bit. Mr. Johnson has only been working at his school since winter break, and so far, Ethan likes him. The girls all have crushes on him because he has an English accent and they think he looks like a young Will Smith. Ethan doesn't see it, though no question his teacher's chiseled body is something to aspire to.

"I think you should try out for the soccer team. I've been watching you run and pass the ball. You'd make a good midfielder. What do you think?"

Ethan stares at him. Nobody ever asked him to join a team before.

"Do you want to play?" Mr. Johnson says.

Part of him really wants to say yes, but he knows he can't do it. Even before all this started, Ma was against after-school sports. *It's no good taking time away from your schoolwork,* she always said. A job is going to interfere with schoolwork too, but it seems he doesn't have a choice about that. "Sorry, I'm not interested." He doesn't say *I can't do it* because Mr. Johnson will ask why.

"Really? The team could sure use your help."

"My homework takes a lot of time."

"I talked to your teachers. They say you're doing well, especially in English class. They thought you could handle a sport, no problem."

"Look, I just don't want to, okay?" Frustration pours out of his shaking voice.

Mr. Johnson narrows his eyes like he's trying to read what's going on in Ethan's head. "Sure. Your choice. But maybe consider it a little longer? I think you'd have fun. I'll ask you again in a few days." He gives the boy a firm pat on his shoulders.

Ethan slips past him out the door, wiping the sweat off his forehead with his sleeve. Turning back toward the school's main building, he pushes past the tide of students leaving for the day. By the time he reaches Mr. Flannery's classroom, the halls are mostly empty.

The door is open. A younger boy who Ethan doesn't know is cleaning the whiteboard. Mr. Flannery is at his desk, hunched over papers that he flips through rapidly. He scribbles a mark at the end of the first set.

After hesitating for a minute, Ethan steps into the room and asks to speak with him.

Mr. Flannery raises his head and gazes at Ethan with cool

gray eyes. "Have a seat." He glances back at the boy, who has just finished his job. "You may go now."

The kid grabs his backpack from a table and scurries away before the teacher can change his mind.

Ethan folds into the chair closest to Mr. Flannery. From here he catches a whiff of the cigar smoke that seems to have permanently settled into his teacher's clothing. It's very slight and maybe other kids wouldn't notice, but Ma has always claimed Ethan has a powerful sense of smell.

"How can I help you?" Mr. Flannery says.

Ethan holds his hands together under the desk. "I was wondering if, um, you might know where I can find a job?" He hopes his teacher might know folks with enough money to pay kids to do work for them around their houses.

"A job? Great idea. It's always best to be productive with your spare time."

Relief flows through Ethan. He'd been afraid his teacher would try to talk him out of it, and then he would be no help at all. "It might be hard to get one, though," Ethan says.

"That's why we have the Internet." He takes out his phone. "Jobs for eighth-graders… babysitting… what about that?"

Ethan shakes his head. "I don't have brothers or sisters. I don't think I could do it."

Mr. Flannery scrolls down the list. "Lawn mowing… stop me if any of these sound good to you… housecleaner… newspaper delivery… do kids still do that? House-sitting… dog-walking…"

"Dog-walking. I love dogs." He doesn't have one, but he's spent time with a few that belonged to friends. "How do I find someone to hire me?"

Mr. Flannery closes his eyes to think. "There's a woman

in my neighborhood who dotes on her two dogs. I can ask her."

Ethan shoots to his feet. "Thanks, Mr. Flannery."

"You're a very special young man." He says this in his usual bland tone, but since he rarely praises any of his students, Ethan knows he means it. A warm sensation fills him.

"Not just because your writing is so polished," Mr. Flannery continues. "I think you have it in you to make something of yourself."

"I hope so."

"It won't be easy. Not around here. Others will try to pull you down to their level. Don't let that happen. Stay steady on your own path. Leave this place behind as soon as you're old enough. Don't let yourself get caught in the cycle of ignorance and poverty and crime."

Mr. Flannery hasn't spoken to him quite like this before. Ethan doesn't really understand what he's going on about, and he doesn't care much for the way his teacher has reduced his home city to its worst possible characteristics. He knows there's also plenty to celebrate about where he lives.

But the important thing is that Mr. Flannery has agreed to get him a job.

Chapter Twelve

IN THE EVENING after Ethan returns from talking to his teacher, Ma makes them bean tacos for supper. After they sit down, she pauses and looks him in the eyes. "I lost my job."

"How come?" He decides there's no point in telling her he already knew.

"Oh, that Cecelia never did like me. She told the boss how I sometimes give you extra cheese or fries. He secretly watched me last time. You're my kid, for heaven's sake. I can't watch you go hungry and not do something about it. With the little they pay us, they ought to look the other way when we feed a little extra of their crappy-ass food to our children."

"It's not fair. You're a lot better worker than Cecelia. She always looks like she's going to bite my head off," Ethan says.

Ma sighs. "The boss likes her, and I can guess why. Nothing I can do. But we're going to be okay." Her voice is upbeat though her eyes tell a different story. "I went to the unemployment office today."

"They going to pay you?"

"It takes a few weeks before it starts. And it won't be the same as what I was earning. It's going to be less." She glances around the apartment. "We're going to have to move. We'll save money in a one-bedroom or a studio."

"A studio?" Having to share a room with his mother is not how Ethan was picturing his high school years. "Maybe we can move in with Aunt Yakeera." She lives nearby and has two bedrooms. The sisters ought to be able to share, and then he could still have his own space.

"What? You can't tell your aunt any of this. She'll just come in here like she always does and try to boss me around. Lecture me on all the shit I did wrong. No way can we live with her. Promise me you won't say anything about me losing my job."

He should've known better than to bring up Aunt Yakeera. His mother had a love/hate relationship with her sister. If Yakeera ever needed anything, Ma was there for her. But she hated when it was the other way around. *Too much pride.* All their lives they had vied to be the best looking and the most talented sister.

"I talked to Mr. Flannery, and he said he can get me a job walking dogs," Ethan says to change the subject.

Ma gives him a wistful smile. "That's good, baby. Every little bit helps."

"It won't be much to start. But once it gets going… once I get some more customers… it might really make a difference."

She tears up. "You're the best, baby. I love you. And I'll get a new job soon." Her gaze sweeps to the electronic keyboard in the corner, her prized possession. "I'm going to practice my singing. I've been away from it too long."

Three years ago, she was a backup singer for a talented

rap artist who might've gone far if his drug problem hadn't caused his career to crash and burn. Maybe she can find something like that again, but it won't be easy, especially now that she's older.

She reads the doubt in his eyes. "Have faith in your momma, boy."

A FEW DAYS later he's on his way to the interview with Ms. Paladino, who's Mr. Flannery's neighbor. She lives in the next city over and Ethan will have to take the train to get there. Plus, he'll have to walk or ride his board to and from the train. He can see this will eat up a lot of his time unless he can find some other clients in the same area to make the trip worthwhile. If things go well, maybe she'll recommend him to her dog-owning friends.

Before leaving the apartment, he washed really well and put on his best clothes. He can still smell Ma's perfumy soap on him. When he reaches the lady's neighborhood, he's glad he put in the effort. It's pretty deluxe, no apartment buildings or retail stores, just all houses, and not the kind that look exactly like each other either. They all have lush green lawns and flowers blooming everywhere and sturdy old trees. Ms. Paladino's home is one of the nicest, bigger than most of the others and with the fanciest garden.

He checks himself and brushes off his pants before ringing the bell, which triggers two sets of high-pitched barking inside.

"Coming!" Seconds later, a woman flings open the door. "Shush, my pretties," she tells the mini-dogs at her feet. They stop barking, but one continues to emit a low growl.

"Hi, I'm Ethan," he says, taking the initiative.

"I'm Terry." The woman is plus-sized with clothes that look custom-fitted. Her blond shoulder-length hair is so smooth it could be a wig. "Come in." She and the dogs lead him to a chair.

"May I pet them?" he says.

"Oh yes, they're very friendly. That's Froo-froo, and this one's Diana."

He lets Froo-froo sniff his hand while Diana hangs back. "Good girl," he says.

"Froo-froo is a boy."

"Sorry. Good boy." At this point both dogs are crowding next to his legs, wanting to be pet. "They're really sweet."

"I think they like you. That's good. Have you been a dog-walker before? You're younger than I thought."

"Um, no. But I'm good with my friends' dogs."

"You don't have one of your own?" She frowns.

Ethan thought Mr. Flannery would've told her about him in advance. That was the whole point of getting a recommendation.

"Oh that's fine. I'll show you how to do it. We'll walk around the block together so you can see their favorite route. You must be careful not to let them eat anything on the sidewalk. Of course, you have to clean up their poo. And don't let anyone pet them." She has several more instructions before she finally finishes.

The walk around the block is awkward, with Ethan trying to hold the dogs' leashes while they pull in opposite directions, and Ms. Paladino issuing frequent commands from behind like a drill sergeant.

"I told your teacher he ought to get a dog," she says. "He said he prefers cats."

Ethan would've guessed that about him.

At the end of their walk, she offers Ethan the job. It doesn't pay much, though. He tries not to think about how many more customers he will need in order to come anywhere near replacing Ma's income with his own.

Chapter Thirteen

THE VELVETY TONES of Ma's voice seep out into the hallway as Ethan lets himself into the apartment after school. Though he would prefer if she were out applying for jobs, he can't help feeling comforted by Ma's flawless rendition of *Cry Me a River*.

She smiles at him and continues practicing her favorite songs, while he goes to his room and gets cleaned up for his first day on the new job. He puts on his plaid button shirt that doesn't need ironing, his newest jeans, and his hardly used gray rain jacket. When he comes out of his room, Ma steps away from the keyboard and raises her phone.

"Look at you. Let's take a picture," she says.

"No time. Gotta get to my job."

"I know, baby. Your first day is a big deal. C'mon now. Stand by the window."

He rolls his eyes before moving in place.

"It's too bright," she says. "Try the wall."

He hurries to the new position. "Ready."

She snaps his picture. "You look too worried. Big smile now."

He's too nervous to pose. She takes several more photos till she gives up on getting a proper smile out of him and sinks down into the armchair. "All that singing wore me out. Will you get me some cheese and crackers before you go?"

"You're making me late, Ma." But still, quick as possible, he prepares her plate and brings it to her with a glass of water.

"Thank you, my lovely son. Now go, make your mother proud."

He grabs his backpack and rushes out. It might be that she calls out for him as he heads down the corridor, but it's too late, he barely has time to get to the train, and she'll manage fine without him. He just hopes she doesn't hit the booze again.

Outside, the drizzle that started earlier has transformed into pelting rain. He jogs toward the station, splattering puddle water all over his good shoes and pant legs. Meanwhile his phone buzzes and he looks to see if it might be a text from Ms. Paladino telling him not to come because of the downpour. But he doesn't have a solid grip on it, and suddenly it's sliding out from between his wet fingers and flying into the street. He leaps out to get it but a car speeding toward him forces a retreat to the sidewalk.

By the time he's able to retrieve it, more than one car has run over it. The phone is smashed. He shoves it back into his pocket and runs the rest of the way to the station, arriving in time to watch the train leaving without him. It'll be fifteen minutes at least till the next one comes.

He looks at his phone but it's beyond repair. He can't get even the simplest function to work. This day has gone from shitty to complete disaster. He can't even call to let his new employer know he's going to be late. He leans against the wall, drenched and shivering, while he waits.

The train doesn't come for twenty-five more minutes. After it arrives at his stop, he sprints all the way to Ms. Paladino's house. At the front door, he stares down at his bedraggled self and prays she'll understand. Over here, the sun is shining and the streets are dry like it hasn't rained one bit. *Rich folk even get the best weather.*

His new employer takes a few minutes to answer his ring. The dogs must be in another room because he doesn't hear them bark.

"Yes?" Ms. Paladino says, looking like she doesn't even know him.

"I'm really sorry. The train was late and my phone broke so I couldn't call you." He shows her the pathetic instrument.

She squints at him. "Looks like you just got out of the bath too. I can't let you in here like that."

"Can you bring the dogs out? I can walk them."

"Sorry, but this isn't going to work. I'm in the middle of a meeting. You should have come earlier." She starts shutting the door.

"Ma'am, please, I really need the work."

"I understand, but I can't just have you popping in any time. I need someone who can be here at the same time every day. The train just isn't reliable when it comes to timing. I'll have to hire someone in the neighborhood." She closes the door before he can say another word.

When Ethan finally gets back home after his miserable day, he finds the apartment looking like a tornado just whipped through it. Drawers pulled out and upended on the floor. The carpet flipped over in the corner. Kitchen canisters tipped onto the counter.

Banging comes from his mother's bedroom. "Ma?" Not till after he calls her name does he think this might be the work of a burglar or worse. His gaze shoots around the room looking for a weapon to defend himself.

"In here!" she shouts back, relieving his worry over an intruder but introducing all new questions regarding her sanity.

He approaches her door and looks in. As he feared, her bedroom is like the rest of the apartment. While he watches, she empties the top drawer of her dresser onto the bed.

"What you doing, Ma?"

She bursts into tears. Throws herself down on the bed. "We have to find all our cash," she says between sobs. "You know how I hide it sometimes? We have to find it."

"Why now? What's going on?"

"They called from the unemployment office. Said I'm not getting shit."

"That can't be right."

"My boss told them I stole from him. I got fired for cause. That means I can't collect unemployment."

"Giving me a few extra fries? That's not fair."

"I don't know what we're going to do."

"You gotta settle down. We'll figure something out." But inside he's thinking, *why have I always got to be the adult?* On the surface, he's calm, but inside it's like all his nerves are tingling, getting ready to do something without having any idea what.

Chapter Fourteen

THE LAST FEW days have been a blur at school. All Ethan can think about is how he and Ma are going to get by without unemployment. At least he managed to convince her she needed to go out and apply for "regular" jobs while she waited for opportunities to reboot her singing career. She's been drinking again at dinner time and sometimes late into the nights, but at least there's been no vodka for breakfast lately.

It's been tough managing without his phone too. They don't have the money to replace it. He can't text his friends; he can't let Ma know when he's running late. He can't look stuff up on the Internet. It's like he doesn't have a life without his phone.

He's been avoiding any conversations with his English teacher since losing the dog-walking job. But when he spots Mr. Flannery in the parking lot after school, heading toward his old-fashioned Chrysler, Ethan forces himself to approach.

"Hello, Ethan." His teacher gazes at him with an unreadable expression, pausing with his hand on the door of his car. Ethan thinks he would make a good poker player.

"Can I talk to you?" Ethan says.

"Not now. I have an appointment."

"Oh, okay, sure, I just wanted to say I'm sorry things didn't work out with your neighbor. You know, the dog-walking. The train was late, my phone broke, I couldn't call her…"

"It isn't like you to make excuses, Ethan. You should've planned on taking an earlier train in case they were running late."

"Yes, sir. Sorry I disappointed you."

"I would think nothing of it if it were another student. But I have very high expectations of you."

"Thanks. I messed up this time, but it won't happen again. Do you know anyone else who needs a dog-walker?"

"I'm afraid not." He gets into his sedan but hesitates before closing the door. "Try Nextdoor dot com. Sometimes people post there when they're looking for services. You might find someone local, and not have to rely on the train."

"Thanks! Only my phone's broken and…"

"Use your computer. I have to run now." He shuts the door, starts the engine.

Ethan waves as his teacher drives off. He didn't get a chance to tell Mr. Flannery he doesn't have a computer. His phone was his computer. His phone was his everything.

He goes to the field and plays some pickup soccer with a few friends from school, trying to get his mind off things. It's getting dark by the time he heads home, so it's surprising not to see any lights in his apartment as he approaches the building.

"Ma?" he calls out as soon as he opens their door. He flips

on switches and checks her bedroom. She's definitely not home, which is odd, because when she has errands to do, she usually completes them in full daylight. He hopes she's not out buying liquor with their dwindling funds.

Ethan assembles some quesadillas for their dinner and turns on the oven to preheat. Just when he's ready to put them in, he hears the key turn in the lock. *Good, she's back in time to eat.*

But when the door opens, it's Aunt Yakeera, not Ma. And from the look on her face, there's something terribly wrong.

"Ethan, I got bad news but your mother is going to be all right."

Right away his hands start to shake. "Where is she?"

"At the hospital."

Oh shit, oh shit, oh shit.

Aunt Yakeera sweeps toward him. "She got hit by a car. But man, my sister is strong. She doesn't have any broken bones! Just cuts and scrapes and bruises. And well, they say she got a concussion. But her head looks all right, she's just a little dizzy." Aunt Yakeera gives him a tight squeeze. "Your momma's going to be all right. They want to watch her tonight, but she should be coming home in the morning."

"How did it happen? Somebody run a red light?"

Aunt Yakeera blows out air. "Doesn't seem that way. Don't say this to anyone, but I think your mother might've had too much to drink before she went out. She tried to cross when the pedestrian light was red. The driver wasn't a bad guy. He stopped, called 9-1-1, stayed by her side till they came. The cops said he felt terrible."

"He should've stopped. There's a person in the street, you're supposed to stop."

"I know, I know. Sometimes people appear suddenly and you don't see them in time, though."

He reaches for his jacket. "I want to go to the hospital."

"No. You stay here with me. She's in good hands right now. We'll get her in the morning. I told her we weren't coming back tonight."

He decides not to insist. After all, he needs to get his homework done. And Auntie said she's doing fine. *No broken bones!* That was amazing. He wonders about the concussion, though. That sounds serious.

MA COMES home at noon on the Saturday after her accident. Ethan greets her at the door but doesn't hug her because she looks unsteady on her feet.

"Who's this handsome young man?" she says.

He's not sure if she's joking or not.

"She'll be loopy for a while." Aunt Yakeera leads her to her room with an arm around her waist. "Confusion is one of the symptoms of concussions. Also headaches and dizziness. She won't be leaving her bed for a few days. I'll get her into her pj's."

"I don't want to put on my pajamas," Ma says.

"C'mon, sister. You'll feel better when you're comfy under the covers." His aunt shuts the door to give Ma privacy while she changes.

Ma's phone rings as soon as Ethan sits in front of the TV. He tracks it to her purse, which Yakeera must've set on the table when they walked in. His first instinct is to bring the cell to his mother, but he pauses, thinking she's in no state to talk to anyone. Since the Caller ID only shows the phone number, he figures it's spam anyway.

On second thought, he answers in case it's someone from the hospital with instructions for her.

"This is Mike Wong from Dealmart. I'd like to speak to Laila Pitt." The man sounds annoyed.

"She's busy. Can I take a message?" Ethan says.

"She was supposed to be here half an hour ago for her interview. You tell her if she isn't here in fifteen minutes, we're removing her from consideration."

"She had an accident. She has to rest for a few days. Can she call you back after that?" Ethan's pulse races.

"Sorry. We need to hire someone now." The man hangs up.

Ethan lowers the phone. He doesn't actually know if she'll be better in a few days. What if she takes months to get over this? By then they'll be evicted. They could end up in the tent city with Uncle Ray.

Aunt Yakeera emerges from the bedroom. "She's sleeping now. I can stay here through the weekend, okay? Help her with the bathroom and stuff. And there's a visiting nurse going to come a few days a week till she's better. You don't have to do it all yourself, Ethan."

He looks down, nodding his head.

"Did you let her boss know she'll be out sick for a while like I told you?"

Since his mother doesn't have a job anymore, he hasn't done that. But he can't tell his aunt because Ma swore him to secrecy. "Yeah, I did," he mumbles, hoping not to be struck dead for lying.

Ethan goes to the library, taking advantage of Aunt Yakeera looking after Ma for the weekend. He has to wait awhile until one of the computers opens up. Following Mr.

Flannery's recommendation, he navigates to the Nextdoor site and looks in the Services Wanted section. Eventually he finds three people looking for dog-walkers in the area.

Once he's got his list, he realizes how bad it will look that he doesn't have a phone where they can reach him. Nevertheless, he goes ahead and emails them to say he's interested, loves dogs, and is very responsible. He hopes they don't want a recommendation from a previous employer, because the only person who ever hired him immediately fired him.

After sending his emails, he hangs around the library for a while waiting for responses. He looks through the shelves and finds a book he wants to read. Then he gets back on the computer to find two out of three have replied.

The first says they already hired someone. The second says they require three positive references and they WILL call them.

Two rejections, and he's already beginning to understand how Uncle Ray must feel, time and again, when someone refuses to hire him. He settles into a bean bag chair and reads for a while before checking his email again.

The third one has replied. Their dog died.

Ethan checks out the book and goes home. There, things go from bad to worse when his aunt confronts him at the door.

"I was going over Laila's papers," she says. "I found a copy of her unemployment application." She glares at Ethan. "What've you got to say about this?"

Ethan's gaze shoots to the bedroom door, which is shut. He lowers his voice. "It's not my fault. She told me not to say anything."

"That's ridiculous. I suppose she's too proud to let her big sister know." She hmphs and haws for a minute. "Might be better this way, though. I doubt that job of hers paid sick leave. At least now she'll be getting unemployment soon."

He probably should tell her that's no longer an option either, but it doesn't seem fair that he's getting stuck with delivering all the bad news. While she rants to herself, he slips away into his own room and shuts the door. He's got enough to worry about without having to deal with the drama between his mother and his aunt.

Later Aunt Yakeera makes them the best dinner they've had for a while. Big juicy hamburgers with ketchup dripping down the sides. While Ma continues dozing in her room, they eat in front of the TV, watching a horror film. Midway through, just as the story is really heating up, he feels Aunt Yakeera's limp hand dropping on his shoulder. He turns and jerks away at the sight of her eyes rolled up in the back of her head, and her snarling mouth open like she's ready to bite.

"Stop!" he cries out.

She laughs. He should not have been surprised, because it isn't the first time she's play-acted during a scary movie. She used to work as an actress and managed to get bit parts in a few low-budget horror films. But when the acting jobs dried up, she turned to hairdressing to support herself. It was sad, he thought… both sisters having to give up on their dreams.

After he goes to bed, sometime in the middle of the night, he's woken by loud groans coming from Ma. She sounds like she's in awful pain. He gets up to help, but when he knocks on her bedroom door, Aunt Yakeera opens it just a crack.

"I got this, honey. Gave her some more Tylenol. Can't give her anything stronger with a concussion. You go back to sleep. I'll take you to church in the morning."

He returns to bed, but it's hard to sleep while Ma is making noises. Not just cries of pain, but it also sounds like she's in a delirium, talking to herself.

How he's going to handle this when Aunt Yakeera goes home, he has no clue.

Chapter Fifteen

ETHAN'S AUNT went back to her own home on Monday. Ma is managing to take care of her personal needs, but Ethan is doing everything else, including grocery shopping, meal preparation, cleaning the apartment, and laundry. She's having more lucid moments again, but they're outweighed by all the time she can't move around because of headaches and stomach upset.

She's supposed to follow the **BRAT** diet for the nausea: bananas, rice, applesauce, and toast. Crackers and bouillon are good too. Mostly she's just not eating, though.

She makes a face when he brings her breakfast in bed.

"You should try to eat, Ma."

"I will, baby." She pats his hand. "I appreciate all you're doing for me."

He leaves for school feeling grateful that the nausea is keeping her from hitting the bottle. He hopes this experience will break her of the habit.

When he comes home to check on her, he finds her sound

asleep in her bed, despite the TV being left on high volume. When he shuts it off, she opens her eyes.

"You want anything, Ma?"

She doesn't answer, just stares blankly at the empty screen. He brings her broth and a banana. "Here you go," he says.

Her gaze shifts to him. "I got to get ready."

"What for?"

"You know. I'm singing tonight with Gold Dog."

This was the rapper she used to work for. But his career sizzled after two years. "Gold Dog's not doing his music anymore," Ethan says.

"What? That can't be."

"It's the concussion. You're not thinking right. You just stay here and get better, okay?"

She makes a face and turns the TV on.

He nods at the food. "Don't forget to eat now."

"I will."

"You'll forget?"

"I'll eat it! Child, what is your problem?"

"It's hard doing everything." There. He said it, and now he feels like a terrible son, particularly since her face shows how much the remark stung.

"Come here." She opens her arms and pulls him into a hug. "I'm sorry, baby. I'll try to be better. I'm going to beat this, and then I'll spoil you like you never been spoiled before."

He draws back. "I have to go out now. I'll be back for dinner."

"Sure, baby." She leans her head back on the pillow.

He heads out of the apartment with his skateboard and rides it to the tent city. He's not sure, but it looks like it might've expanded since the last time he was there. His uncle's tent isn't where it was before and he has to search around until finally he almost trips over it. He shakes the tent flap and calls his uncle's name through the opening.

When there's no response, he repeats, "Uncle Ray? You in there?"

A man with a long gray beard peers out. "There's no Ray here."

"But that's his tent."

"It's my tent. Paid good money for it."

"My uncle must've sold it to you. Do you know where he is?" Ethan's eyes are searching the surroundings.

The man says nothing and retreats into the tent.

"I saw him waiting for a job at the corner of Main and Pine," a woman says behind Ethan.

Ethan turns around. "A job?"

"You know, where the illegals hang out, waitin' for trucks to pick 'em up and drive 'em to construction sites and shit."

"You know when he'll be back?" Ethan says.

"No idea." The woman moves on.

Discouraged, Ethan heads back the way he came.

"Ethan!" Uncle Ray's voice rings out behind him, bringing a smile to his face.

Ethan hurries toward him, though his happiness is short-lived. His uncle is bent over and covered in dirt. Though he tries to put on a cheerful face, he looks as beaten down as any man ever did.

"What happened to you?" Ethan says.

"I've been digging ditches all day. Hey, it's work. I was paid for it."

"You sold your tent."

"I needed the money for food. Things will be better now.

The man who picked me up today says he has more work lined up."

The mention of work gets Ethan excited despite the way uncle looks after a day of it. "You think he'd hire me?"

"You don't want to do work like that."

"I need to do something. Ma's had an accident. She's not gonna be able to do anything for a while."

Uncle Ray stares at him for a moment. "I guess you could try. You'll have to wait for Saturday though. I don't want you missing school. They pick up once a day, eight am."

"I'll be there Saturday."

Chapter Sixteen

ETHAN WORKED on the third chapter of Amari's story early in the morning, inspired by a dream that bees were chasing him. He couldn't sleep anymore after that, probably because he's worried about the upcoming work assignment, which previously left his uncle in such a worn and sorry state.

He puts on his oldest, least-cherished clothes, expecting to end up as filthy as his uncle was, and rides the bus to the intersection where they'll have to wait. Uncle Ray arrives a few minutes later, and they hover amidst other laborers who mostly speak Spanish. Surrounded by an aura of gloom, it feels like waiting to be picked for the least desirable sports team anyone could imagine. But at least they'll get paid.

"I bought back my tent with the money I earned," Uncle Ray says, trying to cheer Ethan with a bit of good news.

A half hour later, many of the men are gone. Uncle Ray begins to despair that the foreman who said he would hire him is not coming. But then he does, and true to his word, he picks Uncle Ray.

"How about my nephew here?" Uncle Ray says.

The man looks Ethan over and laughs. "We can't take children."

"I'm not a child." But Ethan's voice cracks, betraying him.

The man laughs again. "I'll take you but not the kid."

"It's okay, Uncle Ray," Ethan says. His uncle needs the money badly.

"Go on home," Uncle Ray tells him as he climbs into the truck.

"Sure, I will." But after the truck drives away, Ethan remains until the last worker is chosen an hour later. Nobody picks him. He drags his feet back to the bus stop, his pockets empty.

ANOTHER FEW DAYS GO BY, and Ethan's mother is not getting better. She lies in bed or on the couch watching TV when she's awake. More often than not, she's sleeping. The nurse who comes by to check on her every few days says that concussions can last months, if not years. Whenever Ma forgets to take her extra-strength Tylenol, the throbbing headaches return. Then she takes another two for good measure.

Today Ma is more alert when Ethan brings her food in the afternoon. "How is your job going?" Her words are slurred, but he can understand her.

He thought he told her he lost that job, but maybe he forgot. Or maybe it was not a good time to give her bad news then; he can't remember. "It's over. The lady lived too far away. I couldn't get there on time."

Ma blinks with concern. "Lord, I thought you were work

ing. How are we going to manage? What day is it? Is the rent due yet?"

"We still have another ten days," he says.

They won't be able to cover it. The little money they have remaining needs to be saved for food.

"We better sell some things," Ma says.

He glances around the room at the furniture that came from thrift stores, wondering if they could even get five bucks for any of it.

"The TV has to go," she says.

Ethan eyes it, thinking it's so old and small, never mind selling it, they'd probably have to pay to have it dumped.

"Other one too." Meaning the one in the family room.

First his phone, now his TV. Next it'll be his bed and then he'll be sleeping on the ground in the tent city.

She holds out her hand and looks at the two rings she still wears—engagement and wedding. Both have small diamonds.

"No, Ma," Ethan says. "You can't. It's all you got left of him."

"You do what you gotta do."

"Not yet." He doesn't know what to do, though. His uncle can't help them, and Ma won't take anything from her sister. Mr. Flannery hasn't offered any more help. The only time Ethan had a chance to use a computer at school to apply for more jobs, only one person replied, and after they learned he didn't have a working phone, they told him they'd found someone else.

The next day after school, Ethan is headed to the bus when he spots Teshi. He almost doesn't recognize her at first, because she changed her hair and she's wearing a new jacket. The hair is braided and drawn into a ponytail. He knows from Aunt Yakeera that getting a style like that can cost a lot. And the jacket… it looks like suede in a creamy tan color. Paired with some skintight black pants, the girl has never looked so hot before.

That's his first thought; his second is, where's the money to pay for all this coming from? "Teshi!" He springs toward her. She pauses and turns his way, looking at him curiously.

He slows down as he nears her, suddenly feeling self-conscious about other kids watching him run after her like that.

"Hey, what's up?" she says. They step away from the crowd gathering for the bus.

"Um, nice jacket," he says, realizing he needs to work his way up to, *how the hell did you pay for it?*

She smiles and focuses her half-lidded gaze on him. Heat courses through him. *How did she turn sexy, like, overnight?* he wonders.

"You have something you want to say to me, or you just wanted to look at the jacket?"

He tears his thoughts from the unproductive place they were going. "I just, um, was curious. I mean, you've got these fine clothes, and your hair all braided up. What're you doing to pay for all this?"

"What's that supposed to mean?"

"I mean, did you get a job or something?"

"Here I thought you ran over here to ask me out."

A girl laughs behind him, but he ignores her and lowers his voice. "I need to find work. That's why I asked."

Teshi's expression grows more serious. "Hey, I heard about your mother's accident. Sorry. Is she okay?"

"Not really. She can't work right now."

"I get it. Yeah, I think I can help you. But I'm not

supposed to talk about it till I clear it with the boss. He'll wanna meet you. I can set that up and text you later, 'kay?"

"I don't have a phone."

"What?" She looks the same as if he said he lost all his toes climbing Mount Everest.

"It broke. We can't afford a new one right now."

"When did this happen?"

"I don't know. Weeks ago."

"Dude, you need help."

"That's what I said." He lowers his voice. "Hey, this job… it's nothing to do with drugs, is it? I won't sell them. Especially not the hard shit." Weed might be okay, though. He's that desperate.

"It isn't drugs."

"So what is it then?"

"You gotta trust me. Let me set up the meeting." She glances back and sees her bus. "Gotta go."

"Okay, see ya." He knows he should be happy about the prospect of making money. But he's afraid about what he may be getting himself into. Teshi never had any common sense. She's been getting into trouble her whole life. He can only hope this is different.

Chapter Seventeen

ETHAN SETS OUT TO meet Teshi the next day in the late afternoon, lying to Ma, telling her he's going to Chase's house to get help with homework. She'll be passed out in her bed in no time, and she won't know when he comes home or even *if* he comes home tonight.

Teshi is pacing outside. She's tense, nervous, which makes Ethan feel the same way. He's sure now that this must be some terrible shit, and he needs to get out of it. "I changed my mind," he says.

"Whoa, you haven't even heard what I got to tell you. I talked to Antoine—that's the boss. You know what he said? You do this job tonight, and he's gonna give you an iPhone."

"You serious?"

"Yeah, man. Just this once, cuz you need it. It'll be cash pay after that."

An iPhone. Once he's got that, he can get other jobs. That's the main thing that's been holding him back.

Teshi starts walking and Ethan falls in step beside her.

"Where are we going?" he says.

"You'll see."

"You still haven't told me what we're doing."

"You'll find out."

"How am I going to know what to do?"

Teshi turns on her heel and looks at him. "Stop asking questions. It's not that hard. Just do what I do. That's all you gotta do. Do what I do. It'll be over fast." She continues walking, upping the pace.

Ethan is still worried. "I'm not going to hurt anyone, if that's what this is."

Teshi coughs out a laugh. "Are you fucking kidding me?" She pats herself down. "I'm not packin'. You packin'?"

"No."

"So, you think someone would hire us to do a hit? Two fucking kids who don't have a gun between them?"

"Maybe they're going to give us some when we get there?"

"Listen to me. I swear on my dead grammy's body, there won't be guns. We're not killing anyone. We're not even punching anyone. It's not like that."

Ethan believes her. It's true, who would be crazy enough to hire two inexperienced kids to take somebody out? They'd be bound to screw it up. Still, inside he decides that if he gets a bad feeling about this, or sees any weapons, he will run as fast as he can away from the situation. They might kill him but he couldn't hold up his head ever again if he hurt someone.

After about twenty minutes they come to the corner of an alley and Teshi tells him they need to wait there. It doesn't take long before a car drives up and stops in front of them. Teshi gets in shotgun and Ethan slides in the back.

The man who's driving gives him a broad smile in the rear-view mirror. "Hey, Ethan. I'm Antoine." He has a subtle accent Ethan can't place. He's got stubbles that aren't quite a beard, and greasy, salt-and-pepper hair pulled back tight into a short ponytail. He looks old to Ethan, at least fifty or sixty.

"You nervous?" Antoine pulls out into the street.

"A little."

"That's okay. Everyone is the first time. You'll do great. Just do as Teshi does and you'll be fine."

"Okay, I'll try."

"I knew you would. You look like a nice kid."

"Thanks."

"Teshi tells me you need a new phone. You do this job right, you'll get one. Yeah? That'll be your first pay check. Good, huh?"

"Yeah, that's good." A lot better than the twenty bucks or so he had been expecting before Teshi told him. A new phone is worth a lot more than that. And Antoine is right, that's what he needs most of all. Can't do anything else without it. But at the same time, a little alarm is ringing inside him, telling him that if he's getting paid so generously, there's something wrong with this job.

"Try to relax," Antoine says. "We'll be driving a while first." He swivels his head to throw Ethan another smile. There's no warmth behind it, and it dissolves quickly. Then he starts some music—Drake—and nobody talks.

About thirty minutes later they turn off the freeway, some place Ethan's never been before. Antoine drives around for a while before they come to a downtown area. He parks near the front of a café that has outdoor tables.

For a while, he and Teshi just stare at the place. Nothing happens, as far as Ethan can tell. It's not crowded, and since the weather's nice, some customers are sitting outside. There's one couple, and two guys alone on their computers.

At a nod from Antoine, Teshi turns back to Ethan. "Hey. You and me are gonna go in here but we're not staying long. Just do what I do, okay? Antoine will be waiting for us. Afterward, get in the car fast as you can. Okay?" Teshi hands him a baseball cap. "Wear this and pull your hood up over it." She had told him in advance to come in a hoodie. She does the same with her cap and hoodie.

Ethan is pulling on his wristband real hard. "I need to know what we're doing."

"You're doing what Teshi is doing, yeah?" Antoine says. "That's all you got to know."

This is bad, he's sure of it now. "I don't want to," he says.

Antoine twists around to stare at him with cold eyes. "Can't change your mind now. That wouldn't be fair. We're counting on you."

"Please, can you just bring me back home?" He realizes how like a child he must sound. But he is a child. A stupid, foolish child.

"No can do. You're a part of this now. You've met me, seen our methods. You have to put your skin in the game. Otherwise, what's to stop you from squealing on us?"

"I won't! Teshi knows I won't."

"What do you say, Teshi?"

She shifts in her seat. Her eyes don't meet Antoine's. *She's fucking scared of him*, Ethan thinks. She shrugs her shoulders.

"Teshi!" They haven't been friends for a while but Ethan still hadn't expected betrayal.

"Just do it, man," she says.

"Listen to your friend. You're making a big deal out of

nothing. Give it a try, yeah? Then if you don't want to do it again, no problem."

Ethan wants to say no. He wants to demand Antoine drive him back home right now. He wants to tell both of them to leave him alone after that and never contact him again.

But he knows he can't do that. At best, Antoine would kick him out of the car and leave him here. How would he get home? He doesn't even have a phone to call anyone. Even if he could reach his mother, she wouldn't be able to get him. They don't have a car. They don't have money for a taxi.

So he puts on the cap and draws his hood over it. Antoine gives him a big empty smile. "You can do this, kid. I trust you. Just follow Teshi."

And he does. Teshi gets out of the car and Ethan is right behind her. They walk up to the restaurant and she leads him to the front window where there's a menu posted. They both stare at it like they're trying to decide if they want to eat here.

Teshi shakes her head. "Let's try somewhere else." In a much lower tone, she says to Ethan, "You got Baldie."

Perplexed, he glances around and sees that "Baldie" must be one of the two guys working on their laptops. Meanwhile, Teshi weaves her way past the other guy. Acting fast, she snatches the guy's laptop, then races back to Antoine's car.

Cold fear grips Ethan. He knows what he's supposed to do. He isn't even really surprised. He hates himself for it, but he knows he'll do it. The alternative is worse. Antoine will drive away, leaving him here to be arrested for a crime he didn't even commit.

Though it seems like he's been frozen in place for some seconds, it really only takes an instant for him to make his decision, race to Baldie—who's distracted by the first theft—and rip the laptop out from under his hands. Afterward he hurls himself into the backseat of Antoine's car.

Teshi lets out a whoop of joy. "Dude, you did it!"

The car takes off.

Chapter Eighteen

NO ONE TALKS during the drive back from the robbery.
Ethan is too frightened to say anything, and too angry at
himself for getting caught up in something like this. What if
he gets arrested and thrown into juvey? They might even stick
him in regular jail. He could die like his father. What will
happen to Ma then?

He should've known it was something like this. Teshi
always had bad judgment, which was why Ethan stopped
hanging with her. In fact, this exact thing happened when
they were ten years old and went into a Seven Eleven
together. After they came out, Teshi pulled bags of candy out
of her deep pockets. Candy she hadn't paid for. That was the
last time they did anything together until now.

He wonders if she checked for cameras before going
ahead with the steal. Every place has cameras nowadays.
Since Ethan hadn't been sure what they were going to do, he
hadn't looked for them. For all he knows, one was staring
straight down into his face. He feels like he might throw up.

When they get back to their own hood, Antoine pulls into

a parking space. He reaches past Teshi into the glove compartment and takes out an iPhone. "You did good, kid. Here's your reward." He hands Ethan the phone. "Call it a sign-on bonus, yeah?" He laughs at his own joke. "You need this for the job. Gotta be ready when I call. It's a burner, nobody gonna trace it."

Ethan stares down at the phone. Under any other circumstances, this would be the happiest day of his life. He never had an iPhone before. It truly is worth much more than he ever expected to earn.

But he can't rejoice. He sees this thing in his hand, not as a coveted object, but like a ball and chain that will bind him to Antoine forever.

"Aren't you going to thank me?" There's mockery in his tone. He knows exactly where Ethan's reticence comes from.

"Thanks," Ethan says. "Can we go now?"

"What's your rush?" Antoine laughs again. Then he takes out his own phone, opens up a photo, and shows it to Ethan. It's a crystal-clear shot of him running from the café with the laptop in his hands. His breath catches in his throat.

"Nice picture, yeah? People say I'm good at photography. Looks just like you."

"Why'd you take that picture?" Ethan knows he shouldn't ask, but can't help himself.

"Insurance," Antoine says. "Always gotta have a little insurance. I go down, we all go down. I got a lot of these in a safe place." He glances at Teshi to remind her too.

Antoine pockets his phone. "But we don't need to worry about that. You're a good kid, I can see it. Good at doing what you're told. And see, it wasn't that hard. In and out, you grab something and run. I drive us away. Nobody gets hurt. Rich assholes have to share the wealth, that's all. Why should they get everything and nothing for us? We're just taking what we deserve."

"Yes, sir," Ethan mumbles.

"Hey, we're not formal around here. You call me Antoine."

"Okay."

"Okay who?"

"Okay, Antoine."

"Okay. Get outta here now. Both of you."

Ethan has never opened a door so fast. Teshi grabs her backpack and follows him out. Antoine guns it down the street.

"I should've never gone with you," Ethan says.

She pats his arm. "Dude. I got you a phone. Where's the gratitude?"

"It won't stop, not ever. We'll have to steal for him our whole lives."

"It's not so bad. I kinda like it."

"You kidding me?"

"You didn't feel it? The rush? I'm tingling all over right before I snatch the thing. And then, like, my whole body goes electric. Running into the car and Antoine laying on the gas to get us out of there. It's like, I don't know, jumping out of a plane or something."

Ethan doesn't see it that way. Not at all. He's all fear, no excitement. But it's hard not to love Teshi at this moment. Her smile and the way her eyes lit up. She looks more alive.

She pinches his arm. "You wanna do something else?"

"No more stealing," he says.

"No, this is different. C'mon!" She grabs his hand and pulls him behind her.

He knows this is probably another bad idea. Yet he can't

resist her. He's starting to feel exhilarated too. He stole some-thing and got away with it. He must be invincible.

They hurry down the block and Teshi leads him across an empty lot to a dark section behind a warehouse building.

"This looks good." She takes off her backpack and opens the top. "What color you want?"

He looks at her curiously.

"I got red, black, and green." She lifts out the black spray can to show him.

"Shit." He looks around, but the place is empty. "Fine, give me the green."

She hands it to him. "Let's get started."

"What're we doing?"

"Making our mark. Lemme think. What's that dude, you know, the African boy in that story you wrote?"

"Amari?"

"Right." She sprays in a clear spot, making an "A."

"What should I do?"

"I'm doing the writing. Do a picture. Whatever you want."

He looks down at the green can and gets an idea. He sprays above where the writing is going. At the same time, he keeps an eye out for cars.

Teshi switches to red and makes the "m" in Amari look like a heart, then she continues with black again.

"Car," Ethan says. They watch as headlights pass the empty lot. When it continues on past the intersection, they go back to their painting.

"Oh look at that." Teshi stops again, staring at Ethan's picture. "Four-leaf clover. That's dope."

"Could use some of that good luck right now," Ethan says.

He finishes the clover at about the same time as she finishes her sentence: *Amari was here.* "This here's our mark now. 'Amari was here' with a four-leaf clover. We can put it everywhere."

Ethan's not sure he wants to make a career out of being a graffiti artist any more than he wants to steal shit. But he says nothing to dull her enthusiasm.

Another car turns down the street and seems to slow as it nears the empty lot.

"Let's get out of here," Teshi says.

They throw the cans in her backpack and slip away into the darkness past the side of the building. When they reach the sidewalk, they slow down again, not wanting to look like they were up to anything criminal. Ethan walks her to her apartment, which is just around the corner from his.

"You're cool." Teshi pops a kiss on his lips, taking him by surprise, before dashing into her building.

That kiss almost makes everything that happened tonight worthwhile.

When he reaches his own place, he wonders what the hell he's going to say if Ma is awake and in her right mind.

He needn't have worried. She's sleeping soundly in her bed. He shuts off the TV and gets under his own covers quickly. But sleep is a long time coming.

Amari

<h1 style="text-align:center">Chapter Nineteen</h1>

AMARI LOPES *across the open plain with the sun beating down on him. He wants to stop to drink from his gourd, but this water is all he has and it might be a long time before he can find more.*

He must keep up this pace because he delayed too long before starting his pursuit. At least it is easy to track the invaders who captured all the people of his village except for him. They trampled the main road worse than a herd of rhinoceroses. Deep footprints everywhere, broken branches, and human waste mixed in with dirt and grass.

At midday, Amari finds the invaders' abandoned camp from the night before. It includes the remains of several fires, the bones of the animals they ate, and more human waste. He glances through the area without finding anything useful and is about to leave when he spots what looks like a person lying at the far end of the clearing.

His heart sinks when he sees it is Esi, the older sister of his best friend. From her state, it is clear the invaders violated her before killing her. Amari's blood boils with the desire for vengeance. He raises his spear, shakes it at the sky, and shouts out curses against the cruel demons.

He cannot leave her like this. It goes against all the teachings of his culture. Even if he went on to rescue all his people, they would still turn their backs on him for the crime of not performing the burial rites.

He searches for the softest ground before digging a shallow grave using a sturdy branch and his own hands. The sun is low by the time he finishes. He has to drag her body there since he does not have the strength to lift her. When he has gotten her in the grave, he takes his precious gourd and drips water onto her forehead and two hands, while reciting the words he remembers. The rite is not perfect but it will have to do. Then he pushes the dirt back over her, turning away in sadness as he covers her face.

After all this, he eats a strip of dried meat from his dwindling store and runs again. He follows the invaders' trail as long as light remains. Along the way he sees smoke from another village and considers going there to beg them to replenish his food and water. But some in these parts are known to be spiteful, and he does not dare chance that they may hurt him.

When he can no longer lift his feet to take any more steps, he settles in thick grass near the road and instantly falls asleep. He does not wake until the sun is high above him.

When he looks around, he discovers that his spear, his food, and his water are gone. There is no sign of the thief, who probably came from the nearby village.

His throat is parched, his belly empty, and his hope withered.

Chapter Twenty

AMARI HAS *no hope but to go to the nearby village, since he will not get far without water and food. When he arrives, no one pays him much attention. All are busy with the daily tasks of village life.*

He asks to speak to the village elders and is directed to them. He tells them of the theft during the night and asks for their help in finding the culprit and restoring what was stolen from him. But they are old and lazy and do not want to be bothered. "What you describe is nothing unusual," they say. "Every man owns a spear, a water jug, and food."

"But my father's spear is inscribed with the marks of our ancestors," Amari says.

"Go, it is time for our meal," they say irritably.

Amari wanders through the village hoping to spot his father's spear, but hardly anyone carries a weapon. They must all be tucked away inside their huts.

By late afternoon his throat is parched. He approaches a mother for help. "May I drink a bit of your water?" he begs.

"We have had no rain for thirty days," she says. "I cannot allow my children to go thirsty. But I will spare you two sips."

She hands over her flask and he is careful not to take more than what was offered. "Do you know of work I might find in the village to earn food, water, and a spear?"

A man who has been listening speaks up. "Our honey gatherer is ill. Can you gather honey for us?"

Amari hesitates because he has never done it before. But he has seen the honey gatherer work and knows how it is done. "Yes, I will do that," he says.

This is how he finds himself climbing the tree to the hive hanging high above the plain. The action is difficult as he carries a lit branch for smoking out the bees, a curved blade for cutting into their hive, and a bucket for catching the honey as it drains out.

He manages to perch above the hive and begins waving the branch at the bees. But suddenly the entire stick lights up—it must have been too dry—and the flames spark his long hair, which is hanging down over his shoulders. He cries out and drops everything—the branch, the bucket, the blade—and bats his head with both hands to put out the flames. He loses his balance and his foot kicks the hive. The bees race out and begin a mad stinging frenzy against the intruder.

Amari slides and falls down from the tree, banging himself up, but still managing to get to his feet and run. He runs all the way to the mud hole with the bees following and stinging all the way. He throws himself under the dirty water, holding his breath for as long as he can. Finally, the bees go away.

But when he comes out from the mudhole, he sees an angry male rhino staring at him. The rhino must have thought the hole belonged to him. He gives chase.

Amari runs for his life to another tree and climbs up it just before the rhino raises his horn to spear him. The rhino misses him by inches and continues waiting at the base of the tree for Amari to come down.

The sun has set now. Amari is stuck hanging onto branches the whole night long while his body burns from the stings of the bees, and his stomach cries out for food, and his parched throat still has not had a proper drink for two days, unless one counts the mud-filled water he accidentally swallowed.

Chapter Twenty-One

BY DAWN, *the rhino has left, and it is safe for Amari to climb down from the tree. He makes his way back to the mudhole to sip water as well as he can, because he does not know where else to find any. When he has drunk enough to satisfy his thirst, he returns to the village. He still has no food to sustain him for the rest of the trip to the coast, where he must stop the slavers from getting away with his family and the other villagers.*

He has decided he has no choice but to beg for what he needs. In his village, this was considered shameful, and he hopes his family will never learn of it. But he is desperate.

He stands on a corner along the main passageway through the village, and asks for the currency of the village, or food, or anything he might barter. He offers to work for whatever they give him. But instead of earning anything, he is jeered by the village folk, who have heard the story of his setting himself on fire in the tree, being attacked by bees, and nearly killed by the rhino.

At the end of the day, when his throat is parched and his stomach crying out for food, a girl of about his own age approaches. She is very thin with large, angelic eyes, and dirty hands. She wears ragged clothing and her feet are bare. Yet she offers him her gourd of water with only a few sips remaining, and a hunk of bread.

Amari drinks a single sip and returns the gourd so that she may have what remains. He tears the hunk of bread and hands back half of it. They devour the bread hungrily.

"I am Panya," she says.

"Amari," he says.

"I am an orphan. The people in this village are not kind. If we want something from them, we must take it."

"You mean steal?"

"Shhh." She presses her warm fingers over his lips. "Will you help me?"

He never wanted to be a thief, but if he is to survive long enough to rescue his village, he must do what is required. He follows Panya through the village until she places a hand on his chest to stop him.

A necklace has been left hanging outside someone's hut. No one is around, and before Amari can say anything, Panya has run forward and taken it. Both of them race away from the hut without being seen. Amari thinks of the thief who stole his father's spear and blames himself for being no better.

Outside the village, they come upon a trader and offer the necklace for sale. In return, they ask for whatever food and water the trader can supply them with. The trader, sensing a bargain, gives them food and water to last several days.

They set out from the village before they can be caught for the theft, and walk on the main road through most of the night. Finally, when the sky is growing lighter with the approach of dawn, they find a place to lie down out of sight of passing travelers. They eat a bit of the food and drink a bit of the water before curling up together and falling asleep.

Amari's dream is full of nightmares of how he will be punished for his thievery by being cut up into many small pieces.

Rebecca

Chapter Twenty-Two

A FLASH of blinding sunlight hits her and Rebecca feels rather than sees that she's behind the wheel of a moving vehicle. A few blinks and her sight returns, just as the car careens toward the edge of the road. *There's no fucking guardrail.* Only a few yards of scrub grass before the landscape plunges toward rocks and ocean below.

She shrieks, wrenches the wheel to the left, and veers dangerously into opposing traffic. A cement truck bears down on her, its horn thundering. She swerves back toward the cliff, her sweaty hands struggling to keep a grip. The truck hurtles past her, nearly swiping her side mirror. She pumps the brake, struggling to steady herself, until she's got the car under control. Her heartbeat races.

Rebecca pulls into the next turnout and cuts the engine. Lowers her head to the wheel, taking slow breaths to stop the trembling. She screams out a string of expletives.

When she's calm enough to think again, she pieces together how she ended up here. She has just begun a mindcast back to the day Ethan Pitt disappeared. Thinking she wasn't doing anything in particular then, she set her thoughts to land a few hours before he will be seen for the last time. But now she recalls she went to Half Moon Bay to visit her old friend Chi-Ling that day. Arriving early with time to spare, she drove along the coast to enjoy the rare fog-free view.

Mindcasts are disorienting enough without landing in a moving car at the edge of goddamn Highway One. But she doesn't have time to dwell on this. She's farther away than she expected to be. She'll need to drive fast to give herself time to stop at her old apartment and change her clothes before heading to Ethan's. She restarts the engine and merges cautiously back into traffic, planning to escape this death trap of a road as soon as possible.

After reaching home, she throws on her oldest jeans with the tear across the knee. Her gray hoody looks too new, so she switches to a faded black. She pokes a hole into one of her sneakers, with the goal of appearing homeless so no one pays her any attention. A worn outfit. No makeup or jewelry. No purse even. Her money and her phone in her pockets.

Since there's no time for a meal, she shoves down cookies and a chunk of cheese. Her cell rings while she's eating, but she doesn't answer. Afterward she finds a message from Chi-Ling, who's worried that she didn't show up for their lunch date, and thinking something may have happened to her, like, say, driving off the edge of a cliff. Rebecca texts her so she won't report her missing; cops searching for her might mess up her plans for the day. *I'm so sorry, but my dad had an emergency and I had to drive to Berkeley. Everything's okay now. I'll call you later to explain.*

That ought to hold her well enough. And if she doesn't believe the story and never wants to see Rebecca again... so what? To paraphrase a well-known saying, the beauty of mindcasting is that *what happens in a mindcast stays in a mindcast.*

Before leaving, Rebecca glances around for a mask to wear before it hits her that the pandemic hasn't happened yet. She's gotten so used to the mask routine, she practically feels naked leaving the house without one. It saddens her thinking how soon the world will change, and how many thousands of lives will be lost. If only she could warn everyone, but that isn't the way a mindcast works.

She reaches Ethan's apartment with time to spare, which is lucky because there's no place to park on his block. Circling the area, she eventually finds a spot on a parallel street some distance away. She speed-walks back, not wishing to miss anything else that might go on outside the boy's home.

Wondering how she's going to lurk without being noticed, she's happy to discover a bus stop from which she can see the apartment building entrance. She settles on the bench beside a little old lady with steel-gray hair and a large purple tote bag.

There's time for her to take in her surroundings while she catches her breath. Ethan lives in a three-story building shadowed by a tall warehouse across the street. Bars line its first-floor apartment windows, and a plot of weeds welcomes visitors to the front door.

From Ethan's apartment number, Rebecca figures he must live on the second floor, but she doesn't know which way his windows face. She can only hope there's no other way out, or else she might miss his departure. If the information Aunt Yakeera gave her is correct, the boy is inside the apartment right now, warming up soup for his dinner. His mother is passed out in her bedroom, and she won't notice the uneaten bowl he left on the counter till tomorrow morning.

Rebecca only has to observe from outside the building. Either someone came and forced the boy away—her job could be over instantly if that turns out to be the case—or Ethan left of his own accord and she will need to follow him. Hopefully not very far.

That he left without eating his dinner implies something crucial came up, because how long could it take for a thirteen-year-old boy to slurp down soup before going out? This makes Rebecca wonder if a phone call came in from someone demanding to see him instantly. Someone who frightened him.

But according to Yakeera, he didn't have a working cell phone. It had broken some days earlier, and they didn't have the money to get it fixed or replaced. He also didn't own a computer, so he couldn't even have received an email. They still checked his Gmail later, of course, but there were no messages that shed any light on where Ethan went this night.

A bus drives up, blocking Rebecca's line of sight. It remains there several minutes while the old woman uses her cane to creep to the door and up the steps.

Afraid she might miss something, Rebecca walks to the end of the bus to see what's happening across the street. Sure enough, Ethan has come out, and he's already halfway down the sidewalk. His pace is fast, almost a run. He definitely acts as if someone or something has spooked him.

Rebecca struggles to catch up to him without appearing to follow him. An impossible task.

ANY MINUTE NOW, Rebecca is going to lose Ethan. At a brisk walking pace, she's falling behind, but if she runs, he's going to notice her and that could change his behavior. She needs him to do exactly what he did on this night in real-time.

Luckily there's not a lot of pedestrian traffic or she would've lost sight of him already. When she glimpses him turning right at an intersection, she breaks into a jog, but by the time she reaches that street, Ethan has disappeared.

What now? She continues at a slower pace, glancing from side to side. The road is lined with small apartment buildings, interspaced here and there by tiny homes crammed between them. The kid could've gone into any of these places.

At the end of the street, she checks the sign. Oddly, she feels like she's heard the name before but can't recall the context. She hopes it comes to her soon.

In the meantime, she hesitates between continuing in a straight direction without knowing if he turned again, or returning the same way back to her car. It was ridiculous of her to have imagined she might solve the case with one mindcast. Obviously, it's going to take longer and she just needs to be patient. Next time she can simply wait on this street until Ethan shows up. She'll continue trailing him, and even if she loses him every few blocks, she'll mindcast for as many days as it takes to learn where he's going.

But then as she turns to retrace her steps, she spots Ethan rushing out of a narrow residence on the opposite side of the road.

"Don't go!" someone shouts. Her voice sounds familiar, and Rebecca finds out why as soon as the woman darts from the house. *Aunt Yakeera.* Of course, the street name Rebecca recognized. Yakeera had given her the address.

Even in bare feet and a bathrobe, the woman is beautiful, with long, wavy hair draping her shoulders. "Ethan!" she shouts.

He pauses without looking back at her, his face pinched in anger. She runs up behind him and says something at a lower volume than Rebecca can hear. When he tries to leave again, she grasps his arm and speaks urgently into his ear.

After she lets go, he grudgingly gets into the passenger seat of the car parked in the driveway. Yakeera disappears back into the house.

It looks as if they're going somewhere. If so, Rebecca will definitely lose his trail. She won't have time to get back to her own car to follow them.

Sure enough, Yakeera returns fully dressed and carrying her purse. She gets into the driver's seat, and one minute later they're passing Rebecca and she has no way of figuring out where they're going.

She should've known it wasn't going to be easy. *You can't trust anyone to tell the truth.* Not even his own aunt who claims to be desperately seeking him. Her Facebook post that seemed like the only positive movement in the hunt for Ethan, now bears the whiff of something sinister.

Rebecca feels the tingling sensation that often precedes her jump back to real-time just as one more person emerges from Yakeera's house, slamming the door shut behind him. A man with an arrogant expression, maybe in his thirties, tall, blond, and handsome.

She just has time to note the wary manner in which he glances around, and the speed of his departure, both indicators that this isn't his house and he isn't Yakeera's husband.

Chapter Twenty-Three

REBECCA SLEEPS in the next morning. Time travel takes its toll on her, no question about it. When she does finally get up, her hollow stomach cries out for food. She throws on clothes and is about to head to her favorite brunch spot when she sees the mask hanging near her front door. *Damn Covid.* Her favorite brunch spot has been shut down until further notice.

Putting on the mask, she heads to the corner market for eggs and frozen waffles. Later, when she's seated with her coffee and homemade breakfast (if one can call frozen waffles *homemade*), she wonders if she could get used to cooking for herself more often. It certainly would save money.

During her walk afterward, she calls Yakeera. "I have some new information I need to talk to you about. Can we meet somewhere?"

Yakeera cups the receiver and speaks to someone in muffled tones. "Hold on a sec," she tells Rebecca. This is followed by the sound of footsteps and a door closing. "Just getting some privacy. You can say whatever you have to say over the phone."

"Are you worried about the virus? We can sit outside," Rebecca says.

"Of course I'm worried. Aren't you?"

"How about Zoom, then?" If Rebecca can see her face, she might be able to sense whether she's telling the truth.

"We're not Bill Gates over here," Yakeera says.

"Fine. The phone will do. So, I wanted to let you know I've been talking to some folks in the neighborhood."

"What folks?"

"Um, I can't tell you. Confidentiality and all that. But I learned something. Ethan's mom wasn't the last to see him before he went missing."

Rebecca pauses for a response but it's silent on the other end.

"A neighbor saw Ethan run out of his apartment building. So, like, no one snatched him or anything. After that, someone else witnessed him arriving at your house. According to them, he didn't stay long. But then you came out after him and convinced him to get into your car. The two of you drove off together."

Rebecca gives Yakeera a chance to respond, but she appears to have shocked the woman into silence. She continues. "And right after the two of you drove off, some guy my witness had never seen before left your house. Tall. Good-looking. Blond."

"You can't put that in that article of yours." Yakeera has lowered her voice like she doesn't want anyone else to hear. "It's got nothing to do with Ethan."

"You say you care about your nephew. But you had information about where he was that night, and you told no one."

"What difference does it make if he disappeared from his house, or from outside the restaurant? Anyway, it didn't matter to the officer we spoke to. Took him one minute to decide Ethan was part of a gang and it was a rival gang that killed him. That didn't even make sense. Since when do gangs bother to hide the victim? They just shoot each other down—bystanders too—and leave the bodies in the street."

"But it does matter where he was last seen. I need you to be honest with me if I'm going to get at the truth."

There's a deep breath on the other end. "If you promise me nothing about that man is going to be in your article."

Since Rebecca will never write an article, she can make that promise with a clear conscience. "If he's got nothing to do with any of this, you and he have nothing to worry about. I need his name, though."

"I can't tell you that."

Rebecca decides not to press her. "You mentioned a restaurant. Is that where you took Ethan?"

"His favorite place. Dos Amigas. He loves Mexican food."

"Me too. Was there a particular reason for going out to eat right then?"

"I'll level with you," Yakeera says. "Ethan walked in on me and my man. He's married. And his wife has some dough. I don't care about it; I just like having a little fun with this dude. But I didn't want to wreck things for him, so I ran after Ethan and told him we needed to talk. I had to ask him not to mention what he saw to anyone, especially his mom." She lowers her voice to a whisper. "She's a big gossip."

"Did Ethan agree not to say anything?"

"Sure. He's a good kid."

"After dinner, where did you and he go?"

"He didn't stay through dinner. Said he was using the bathroom and didn't come back. I don't know what happened. I assumed he saw someone he knew and went off with them. But that's the mystery."

Rebecca considers for a second. "What about your lover? You say he's got a wife. Maybe he was more upset than you thought about Ethan catching you two together."

"What're you saying? You think my man killed him? That's bullshit. No way."

Rebecca says nothing.

"Don't you go off in that direction. Just find out where Ethan went when he left the restaurant. That's the key. My man's got nothing to do with it."

"Okay," Rebecca says, just to keep the peace. "I'll see what I can find out. One other thing. It would help if you got me a list of anyone who was close to Ethan, with their physical addresses, phone numbers, email addresses. Pictures too, if you have any. I'm talking about relatives, friends, mentors. Anyone Ethan spent time with." She figures this may save her time while she's following the boy around in mindcasts. It would be good to recognize right away if he's meeting up with someone he knows, or if it's a stranger.

"You sure don't ask for much."

"Can't you find that stuff on his phone?" Kids' whole lives are on their phones these days. All their friends. All the websites they visit, the social media where they're active. All the texts and emails right there for anyone to read.

"His phone broke before he went missing. Remember? His mother couldn't afford to get him a new one. It was unusable, so we couldn't even check it to find out who's on his friend list, or who texted him recently."

Rebecca did remember, but she thought there must be other ways to get that information. "Couldn't the police find that out by checking with the phone company?"

"If they did that, they're not telling us," Yakeera says.

"Maybe you can use another phone to access his cloud storage?" Rebecca says.

"Like I said, we're not Bill Gates over here."

"Right." Rebecca isn't exactly Bill Gates either.

"I'm sorry I didn't tell you about the restaurant," Yakeera says. "Ethan's mother and I are grateful for your help. Please, find out what happened to our boy."

Chapter Twenty-Four

THOUGH A YEAR HAS PASSED since Ethan's disappearance, Rebecca feels an urgency to find him. If he's alive, every day might be a fresh new torture. Now that she's begun this search, it would feel like a betrayal even just to pause for a bit. Concern for him has wrapped itself around her heart, squeezing and twisting to goad her into constant movement.

Which is why she dives directly into a new mindcast the night after her phone call with Yakeera. This time she avoids the near plummet off the ocean cliff, and still makes it to Dos Amigas Restaurant before Yakeera and Ethan.

She snags a table beside the window facing the parking lot so she'll be able to see when they arrive. It would've been nice to arrange a spot within listening distance, but even if she'd been able to time her arrival directly after theirs, and even if there was an empty table next to them, and even if she convinced the hostess to seat her there, she probably wouldn't hear their conversation. The restaurant is crowded with families talking (and screeching) at maximum volume, competing to be heard above all the other raised voices.

Rebecca orders an appetizer and a cup of coffee. "Can I pay for this now? I won't be getting anything else." She'll nurse her drink and guacamole for as long as it takes, and then she needs to be ready to leave in an instant.

"No problem." The server wanders off.

Before the food arrives, Yakeera's car veers into the lot and swerves into the first empty spot. She and Ethan spill out and head toward the entrance, the boy a few steps ahead of his aunt. His expression is troubled, his shoulders dipped. It hits Rebecca that this is the last time anyone in his family will see him. Something terrible is about to happen to this child, and she is now tasked with witnessing it. The thought makes her hands shake, causing a few drops of coffee to spill out.

The hostess seats them in the middle of the restaurant, giving Rebecca a view of Yakeera's face and the back of Ethan's head. She's way too far to eavesdrop, unfortunately.

Yakeera does most of the talking and she's quite animated, though that might be her normal state. After they place their order, she opens her purse, fishes inside for a wad of bills, then pushes them across the table to Ethan. He whisks them into his pocket.

Rebecca wonders if she's paying for Ethan's silence in the matter of the boyfriend. She didn't mention doing that. The whole thing strikes Rebecca as odd. Why was it so important to preserve this secret?

Maybe she should go outside and prepare to follow Ethan now. But their food hasn't arrived, and she doubts the boy could summon up the fortitude to give up a free meal at the restaurant his aunt said was his favorite, however much he might need to leave and possibly meet up with someone.

She waits, finishing her chips and dip. When her plate is taken away, she continues to sip her coffee as if she has all the time in the world, though several people in the waiting area are casting dirty looks her way.

When their food arrives, Ethan attacks it like it's going to bolt if he doesn't eat it all first. At this rate, he'll be done in a few minutes. She believes she's witnessed the one significant action here—the handing over of the cash. She gets up to leave.

Outside, she heads toward her Honda in the parking lot. Best to be out of sight when the boy comes out. But as she crosses in front of the restaurant, she notices a man seated in his car watching the dining area. At first, she figures he's just waiting for someone. But on further thought, it seems strange he's doing nothing but staring into the building. When she waits for someone, she does stuff on her phone. Checks email, listens to podcasts, plays games. He's not even holding his phone.

She turns like she's searching for someone in the lot, but actually she's throwing glimpses into his car. There's plenty of light spraying out from the restaurant, plus a nearby street lamp, so when he leans forward just a bit, she gets a better view of his features.

It's the man who was at Yakeera's place. The guy who's sleeping with her.

Her body tingles with excitement. *It must be him.* He has a motive to kill Ethan. He wants to silence the boy.

His gaze shifts to her. *Crap.* She hopes her face didn't reveal the surprise and even fear that she was feeling on seeing him. While the man watches, she pretends to wave at someone in the distance and moves on with determined steps. At the same time, she's getting out her cell, positioning it so that hopefully he can't see it. She clicks a photo of his license plate as she passes.

Continuing toward her car, she glances back and sees his eyes in the rearview mirror. His door opens; he must've glimpsed her taking the picture. Panic fills her as she throws herself into her car, wondering how she'll deal with him if he confronts her.

But then he pulls his car door shut again, starts his engine, and reverses out of his spot. Ethan has just come out of the restaurant by himself, having given Yakeera the slip. Rebecca gets out of her car, ready to follow him on foot.

Boyfriend drives up alongside Ethan, lowers the passenger window, and calls out his name. The boy stops and peers into the car. Looking both surprised and annoyed, he glances around as if seeking a means of escape. But Boyfriend must still be talking to him, and Ethan keeps listening. After several more seconds, he opens the door and gets in. The car takes off.

Crap again. Rebecca dives back into her own car, starts the engine, flings it into reverse, and screams toward the exit, frightening an older couple on their way out of the restaurant.

But when she reaches the street, Boyfriend's car has disappeared. She drives to the nearest intersection and scans in each direction. No sign of them. They're gone.

There's still something she can do during this mindcast, however. She drives a bit further and pulls into a supermarket parking lot. It's 8:45, not too late. She gets out her phone and calls Freddie, the detective who was in charge of the investigation into her sister's disappearance.

He might not be pleased that she's still using his private number. That was for Sadie, but now that she's been found, there's no more excuse for her to have her own direct access to a cop. Still, she hopes he'll understand.

He picks up after three rings. His voice is gruff; maybe she interrupted something. "I hope everything's all right," he says right after greeting her.

"Yeah, yeah, it's all good. Except just this one thing." She wonders if she should have a little banter with him first to lighten the mood, but she feels the tension in his voice and there's no doubt he wants to end this call as soon as possible. "I'm wondering if you can trace a California license plate for me."

Dead silence on the other end. Then finally, "What's this about?"

"A car dinged mine in a parking lot tonight. The asshole left without a note or anything. Jerk."

"How do you know the license plate?"

"Oh, I… well, the car looked kind of sketch, so I glanced at the number on my way into the restaurant. You know, I'm good with numbers. I remember them."

More silence. "It might not even have been that same car."

"Pretty sure it was."

He sighs. "I wish I could help you. But the best way for you to deal with this is file a report with the local police. They should be able to help you. If they're not helpful, you can get back to me."

"Really? That sounds like it will take a whole lot of time."

"It shouldn't. Now, unless there's something else you want to tell me, I need to hang up."

It was her turn to sigh. "Well… if maybe there was some other reason I really need the number, what would you recommend?"

"What other reason?"

It hits her she's still in a mindcast. Whatever she says, Freddie won't remember in real-time. She can afford to take a chance. "It has to do with another kidnapping case."

"Oh boy. Do I have to remind you what happened the last time you investigated a case on your own?"

He is referring to her being left for dead at the bottom of a ravine and just barely surviving. "It isn't like that. This is about a boy who—"

"I'm sorry, I can't condone this. If you have some legitimate information, come talk to me about it and I'll see what I can do. Otherwise, we're done here."

They were definitely done.

Chapter Twenty-Five

2020 - PRESENT

THE DAY after her time jump to the restaurant, Rebecca is planning her next move. Clearly Freddie is not going to be at her beck and call, and she can't really blame him. Sticking her nose into a missing person's case is probably not a safe thing to do, and Freddie, as a police officer, is all about preserving public safety. Plus, he knows her, and knows she'll take dangerous chances when she feels they're called for. He isn't about to make that lifestyle easier for her.

She needs to hire a private eye. Someone who can identify the owner of the car Ethan got into right after leaving the restaurant, on the night he disappeared. It's going to cost her, but she can afford it, for now.

Freddie must've encountered some private eyes in the course of his investigations. It can't hurt to ask. She believes there would be nothing illegal about his telling her the name of someone he respects.

She texts him so that it seems ultra-casual. *Do you know a private investigator in the Bay Area that you can recommend? Asking for a friend.* Hopefully, keeping it light will prevent him from getting concerned about it.

Only a few minutes pass before her phone buzzes with the reply. *Ian Slate*, followed by a phone number. Excited, Rebecca texts her thanks, calls Mr. Slate immediately. and leaves him a message.

He returns her call two hours later. "Ms. Danser?" His voice is a smooth baritone.

"It's Rebecca."

"This is Ian Slate."

"Thanks for getting back to me. I was wondering if you could help me trace—"

"If you don't mind, I prefer to meet with prospective clients in person first."

"During Covid?

"I mean, over Zoom."

"Sure, but it's just a small job at the moment. Might lead to more work, but I don't know."

"That's all right," he says. "No matter how small the job, my policy is to begin with a face-to-face meeting. Old-fashioned, I know, but it's the way I roll."

She hesitates. It seems like a lot of trouble just to trace a license plate. On the other hand, if she needs his services in future it's best to get the meeting part out of the way. "I'm pretty open." *Translation: absolutely nothing is on my schedule.*

"Tomorrow morning at nine?" he asks.

She agrees and after they hang up, Rebecca is left thinking it might be good for her to have a night off from mindcasting. Lately she has been getting headaches. Ibuprofen generally takes care of them, but she does fear they'll get worse if she pushes her body too hard. She doesn't have any way of knowing the long-term effects of traveling through time.

Yet the thought of delaying the search for Ethan even one more day causes a churning inside her.

A FEW MINUTES BEFORE NINE, Rebecca settles next to the small table she set up for Zoom conversations. Thinking that at some point she might need to interview for a job via Zoom, she actually Googled advice on recommended backgrounds and lighting before choosing this spot. Behind her is a blank cream-colored wall and a low shelf. The advice told her not to have anything too distracting in the background or whoever she's speaking to will focus on that instead of her. However, the advice then contradicted itself by suggesting one or two personal items would help to prove she's not a robot. For this reason, she placed a family portrait and a fake plant on the otherwise empty shelf.

However, because Rebecca is an extremely private type of person, the family portrait is not actually of her family. It shows two parents and two daughters, the older of whom looks a little like Rebecca. The daughters are roughly twelve and ten. Anyone who actually knows Rebecca would realize the photo could not be of her family, because at these ages, Sadie was kidnapped and her mother was dead.

The Zoom link arrives precisely on time, scoring one point for the prospective P.I. The connection goes right through, and she is immediately looking at a man of around forty, with his auburn hair and beard neatly groomed. He's quite slender, and it appears he is also tall, though it's hard to judge when the person is seated. Overall, he's like a cross between George Clooney and Andrew Garfield, with the face of the former and the lean physique of the latter. He's dressed with a European flair in a tan blazer over a plain black T-shirt. His neat presentation makes her wish she'd worked a little harder on hers.

After their greetings, he sips from a tiny glass filled with what looks like tea.

"Is that all you're having?" she says.

"The tea? I learned this in Istanbul. It stays hotter when you drink it in a small cup and keep refilling it. I like my tea very, very hot."

"I see. Do I need to tell you about myself, or have you already found out everything?"

"I'm sure you would expect no less of a P.I. Congratulations on the safe return of your sister. You were quite brave to stand up to those kidnappers."

"I wish I had done a few things differently."

"Don't we all. Tell me why it is you need a private investigator after having found your sister already."

She has thought about how she will answer this. "I'm sure you can imagine what it would feel like to have a family member missing for so many years. How you almost wish they were dead because at least then they wouldn't be suffering."

He gives a subtle nod.

"Having felt that for so many years," she continues, "I hate the thought of others going through it. I guess it wasn't enough for me to save my sister. I want to save others who've gone missing too."

"How do you propose to do that, aside from hiring me?"

"I have certain skills. I'd rather not go into that part. Let's just say, I'd like to use your services for the smaller jobs that require access to records and so on. In this case, I'm just looking for someone to trace a license plate number. There could be more jobs later, but I'm not sure. Maybe another case eventually. It kind of depends on how this one goes. Is this worth your while? Right now, I simply need that trace."

"I can do that for you. And I'm intrigued regarding your goals. I'd also like to make better use of my skills. Unfortunately, I mostly get infidelity cases. Although sometimes I help a person who really needs to be convinced to exit their marriage for their own well-being, it's more often an excuse for an overly controlling husband to keep his wife on a leash." He drains the tea from his glass before setting it down. "Can you tell me more about what you're working on now?"

She considers it, then shakes her head. "Sorry. I'm not ready to share. I barely have enough money to support myself and not much extra to pay for your services. At this point I expect to be doing most everything myself."

"All right. I can do this job for you, and if that's all there is, okay. I'll need you to sign paperwork and put down a retainer. If you send me the plate number, I can get on that later today. It won't take long."

"Sounds good." She's distracted trying to read the titles on the bookshelf behind him. It's clear now why the typical Zoom advice says to keep the background empty.

"You love mysteries, I see." She nods toward the books. One row features Sherlock, another, Hercule Poirot. Other classic sleuths are represented too.

"I always wanted to be a detective," he says.

"Do you play the violin?" A case rests at the center of one of the shelves.

"You might say so." Ian Slate seems rather on-the-nose,

from his slick name to his European flair, his mystery collection, and his violin (that his hero Sherlock also played). But she rather likes him for it.

"Don't forget to water your plant," he says before ending their meeting.

She laughs to herself. Was he being sarcastic? She likes that too.

IAN SLATE IS true to his word. He calls a few hours after their meeting with the name of Yakeera's boyfriend—Craig Ballard—and his address and phone number.

"There's something else that may interest you." He sounds pleased regarding whatever he's about to reveal.

"Oh?"

"He's a lawyer turned politician. Running for the California Assembly in 2020."

"Really?" She can't keep the excitement out of her voice. It all makes sense now. Yakeera's story about being worried that Ballard's wife might find out the truth from Ethan did not add up. Even if the boy told his mother, and she blabbed to the whole neighborhood about Yakeera's hook-up with Ballard, how would that ever reach the man's wife? She definitely did not run in the same circles as Ethan's family.

If the man was aiming for a career in politics, though, that was a whole different thing. His opponent would be looking for dirt on him. Rebecca doesn't really know how it all works, but there's no question someone in public office has to be squeaky clean these days, or it's going to come out.

"Does that help?" Ian says.

"It could be related. Thank you."

"Let me know if I can do anything else."

After they hang up, Rebecca considers calling Ballard before rejecting the idea. Too easy for him to blow her off on the phone. She needs to go to his place, and the best way to do it is during a mindcast. She relishes having the power to question him without his even knowing about it in real-time.

Chapter Twenty-Six

2019 - MINDCAST

REBECCA DECIDES on jumping back to a week after Ethan vanished. His disappearance will be public knowledge by then, at least for the tiny portion of the public that knows him. If Ballard is innocent, the details of where and when he picked up Ethan, and where and when he dropped him off, will still be fresh in his mind. And if he's guilty, he'll be more likely to be jumpy about it in these early days and possibly give himself away. He's probably not expecting anyone to connect him to the case, and it might really throw him off when she does.

After landing in the past, Rebecca sets out directly for Ballard's house. She turns up his winding driveway by 6:30 on the Monday evening following Ethan's disappearance. It seemed like a good choice for finding Ballard at home. *Who goes out on a Monday?* Rebecca never did, but then again, she rarely went out any other night either.

The house is a stunning contemporary, high in the hills with a view of the bay. If this place came from his wife's fortune, it gave him even stronger motivation—along with preserving his political career—to keep anyone from learning about his affair with Yakeera.

A Tesla and a Maserati are displayed in the driveway, more signs of their wealth. She hopes it's also a sign that he's home. She parks behind the Maserati and proceeds to the front entrance.

Rebecca rings twice before a woman's high-heeled footsteps approach. The woman speaks through the door. "If you're here to sell us anything, whether it's magazines or religion, you've come in vain."

"I'd like to speak to Mr. Ballard regarding a criminal investigation."

There's a brief silence. She definitely hadn't been expecting that. "Are you a police officer?"

"No, a private investigator."

Mrs. Ballard opens the door and looks her over. "What are you investigating?"

"I'm sorry, but I'm only authorized to speak to your husband about it."

The woman appears to hover between her desire to throw Rebecca out and her curiosity to learn what this is all about. Her curiosity wins. "Wait here."

She takes her time going up the stairs. A few minutes later, Ballard trots down with his wife following. Rebecca recognizes him as the man she saw leaving Yakeera's home.

"Mr. Ballard?" she says.

"Yes." He doesn't offer his hand.

"I'm Rebecca Danser. Could we speak in private?"

He throws a nervous glance at his wife, who directs a cold stare back at him. "Sure," he says. "This way."

He leads Rebecca to a study and closes the door. "Have a seat."

"I'm fine here." She leans against the desk, hoping to be at least a little intimidating in a way that wouldn't be possible if she sunk down into one of the plush chairs.

He also remains standing, probably for the same reason. Since he's taller than she is, it appears he's won the intimidation contest. "What's this all about?"

"A boy named Ethan Pitt. You probably heard he's gone missing?"

"Ethan…? I'm not sure who you mean."

"Yakeera McDade's nephew. I think you know him."

He gives her a puzzled look. "Yakeera, my haircutter? She might've mentioned him; she talks a lot while she's doing my hair. I don't know the kid. I barely even know her."

Unfortunately, he appears to be an excellent liar. Rebecca knows for a fact that Ballard picked Ethan up in his car, and yet he looks like he's telling the truth. Maybe they teach this skill in learning-how-to-be-a-politician school. Or maybe she needs to get better at reading people's expressions. She must find out if there's a class she can take. "Look. I'm not trying to embarrass you in front of your wife. But Yakeera told me she was having an affair with you."

He snorts. "That's a lie."

"Why would she lie about a thing like that?"

"How would I know what motivates her? Maybe someone paid her. Or maybe she's crazy and likes to make up stories about her clients. You know she's a wanna-be actress, right?"

His dismissive attitude only annoys Rebecca further. "You should know I have another witness. Someone who saw you leaving Yakeera's house."

Did that cause a little flinch? She's not sure.

He recovers immediately, however. "Again, this person is

lying. I don't know their motivation. Maybe you should ask them. If you've got nothing better, this conversation is over."

"According to Yakeera, Ethan accidentally walked in on the two of you. And you were worried he might tell others."

"Is that what this is about? You think I did something to stop him from talking? That's truly ridiculous." He steps toward the door.

"Another witness saw you pick him up in your car outside the Dos Amigas Restaurant."

He hesitates. *Is that a line of moisture popping out on his forehead?* But he isn't ready to talk, that's for sure. He opens the door. "I think you know your way out."

Rebecca takes her time crossing the room.

"One thing I do remember," he says. "Yakeera was worried about that kid. She thought he was getting into some serious shit."

"Like what?"

"You know. Drugs. Gangs. Guns. He lives in a tough neighborhood. That's how it goes."

Chapter Twenty-Seven

THE NEXT TIME REBECCA MINDCASTS, she's back to the night Ethan disappeared, waiting in her car outside Dos Amigas Restaurant. This time around, she has not gone into the place at all. When she arrived, she eased backward into the parking spot so she would be ready to drive away at a second's notice.

She saw Ballard arrive twenty minutes ago. Since then, they have both watched and waited; him the mouse, and her, the cat ready to give chase.

She tenses as the restaurant door flies open and Ethan jogs out. The scene replays itself, with Ballard backing up, easing next to him, and the boy getting into his car. But this time Rebecca starts her car and follows them out of the lot.

Tailing Ballard isn't as hard as she thought it would be. Traffic is light, and even in the dark she can distinguish his Tesla up ahead. He doesn't appear to be worried about anyone tracking him. He signals before each turn, obeys the speed limits, and even drives courteously.

She's getting complacent by the time the light turns yellow at an upcoming intersection and Ballard makes it through. Though it's red when she gets there, she's planning to continue anyway, except a line of cars in the green light direction has already started across. She slams on her brakes, barely avoiding a collision. Fuming, she watches the back of Ballard's car as it signals a left turn up ahead.

When she finally gets the green, she floors it to the next intersection, where the red light blocks her again. Ballard is long gone by the time she turns onto the street where she last saw him.

She pulls into a gas station, parks on the side, and bangs on the steering wheel. Tailing a car is much harder than she imagined, especially in the dark. There has to be a better way to find out what happened to Ethan.

WHEN REBECCA first became involved in the search for Ethan Pitt, she had imagined jumping back once, watching him get picked up by someone and figuring out who that someone was. *Voilà!* Mystery solved.

She knows now it's going to be much harder. Although Ballard still appears to be the number one suspect, she could spend forever just trying to tail him across town.

Naturally she had hoped for a quick solution. But this *following people about* no longer feels like the right approach. She needs to dig deeper, to get an understanding of Ethan and his friends and family. It will be a better use of her time to act like a cop or a private eye, by talking to people, hearing what they have to say, drawing out their stories. Then she should have a better understanding of where to focus her energy.

At first, she considered interviewing all the players in real-time. But a year has passed and their memories will be fuzzy. If instead she talks to everyone a week after Ethan has gone missing, their memories will be fresh, their emotions raw.

She should not have waited this long to seek out Ethan's mother. Laila must know her child better than anyone. It has to be possible to glean something from her.

Rebecca's next mindcast brings her to Ethan's apartment building, in the early evening a week after he's vanished. She has put some effort into her appearance for this visit. Unlike her previous time here, when she hoped no one would notice her, she thinks it might help to look like someone successful. Someone who has influence and might make a difference in the search for Ethan. Before coming, she styled her hair and applied more makeup than usual. She put on gold dangling earrings and three small hoops in the upper holes of her left ear. Also bangles on her right wrist. She dresses in the most fashionable outfit she has, basically *older student chic*. The goal is to appear hip, intelligent, and concerned. She has no idea if she's succeeded.

Ringing their apartment buzzer with one hand, and hanging onto a box of blueberry muffins with the other, she waits for an answer. Maybe Laila went out for an errand. It doesn't seem likely she'd be gone long, though. A woman whose child has recently disappeared isn't likely to stray far from her home.

Ten minutes later a man arrives and gets out his key to let himself into the building.

"Excuse me," Rebecca says. "Do you know Laila Pitt? She's not answering her buzzer."

"Laila moved out," he says. "Living with her sister, I think."

"Yakeera?" Rebecca doesn't know if there may be more than one.

"I think that's her name."

"Thank you."

He nods and lets himself in.

Rather than look around for parking again, Rebecca walks to Yakeera's house. The woman doesn't know her yet, which hopefully will be to her advantage.

Yakeera answers her door quickly, beautifully turned out, with flowing hair and large silver hoop earrings. The expert application of eyeliner adds a kind of soulful depth to her toffee-colored eyes. "Can I help you?"

"My name is Rebecca Danser. I'm a freelance journalist. I heard about your nephew, Ethan Pitt. I'd like to do a story on his disappearance and I was wondering if I could talk to you and Ethan's mother."

Her eyes sharpen with suspicion. "What paper are you with?"

"I'm freelance. I don't work for a paper. I write the story and then try to sell it."

"And why on earth would you think any paper would pay money for Ethan's story?"

This conversation feels like déjà vu. Rebecca repeats the same explanation she gave to Yakeera in real-time, how she wants to change things, how it's about time people of color got some respect and attention. Yakeera counters with the same objections as before, but eventually Rebecca's arguments prevail.

Ethan's aunt takes a deep breath before glancing back into the house. "Okay." She widens the door opening. "Come in. We'll see what you've got to say for yourself."

"Here, I brought these." Rebecca hands over her offering of muffins.

"How'd you know I love these?" Yakeera's face brightens.

Rebecca smiles and doesn't say she read it on her social media.

"Would you like some coffee?" Yakeera says.

"No thanks, just water." Rebecca glances around. Classic horror movie posters, beautifully framed, hang from the walls. *Psycho*, *The Creature from the Black Lagoon*, *The Bride of Frankenstein*, and *A Nightmare on Elm Street* are among those Rebecca is familiar with. There are several other films she doesn't know.

"I don't think I've seen this," Rebecca says, staring at the blood-splattered artwork for *The Beast of Hampstead Moor*.

The look in Yakeera's eyes deadens. She raises her arm and points with a limp hand. "May I show you the crypt?" Her voice quavers like a witch's cackle.

At Rebecca's incredulous expression, she laughs. "My one line in that film."

"Oh wow. You just sent chills down my spine. I didn't know you were an actress."

She shrugs. "You know how it is. Unless you break in bigtime, you need another job to support yourself. Probably half the Uber drivers in LA are aspiring actors."

She gestures for Rebecca to sit down. The furniture is simple, modern, and there's not too much of it. Throw pillows and blankets add a sense of warmth to the main room. Dishes are put away, counters wiped.

A petite woman is seated in the corner. Her gaze is on Rebecca, yet her eyes seem unfocused.

"This is my sister Laila," Yakeera says. "Ethan's mother."

"Nice to meet you," Rebecca says.

Laila doesn't reply.

"How are you feeling, honey?" Yakeera says.

Laila nods.

"My sister got a concussion recently. It's been tough for her. Expressing herself is hard. She can listen all right. Have a seat, um…"

"Rebecca," she reminds her.

"Rebecca. Right," Yakeera says.

"Do you mind if I record our conversation?"

Yakeera looks at Laila, who nods.

"It's fine."

Rebecca can't bring a recording back with her to real-time, but she's doing her best to convince them she's an actual professional writer. It also could help her to review the conversation before leaving the mindcast. She sits near Laila and sets up her phone on the table between them.

"Before I start, I just wanted to express my deepest sympathy for what you're going through right now. I also want you both to know that I understand it because I've experienced something similar. My sister was abducted when she was four and has never been found." At this point in time, Sadie is still missing.

Yakeera's face fills with concern as she shifts her gaze to her own sister. Laila too appears saddened by Rebecca's disclosure. *Good.* She hopes this will make them more cooperative.

"I'm really sorry," Yakeera says.

"Can you tell me about Ethan? What's he like? What does he enjoy doing? Who are his friends? And so on."

Yakeera glances at Laila, but it's clear she isn't up to answering something so comprehensive. "I'll tell you what I can. Ethan is the sweetest, most good-hearted kid I know. Yeah, I'm his aunt, but still, if he was a mean little SOB, I would tell you."

"Okay."

"He's never had a lot of friends, has he?" Yakeera looks to Laila for confirmation. Laila shakes her head.

"But it isn't because he's not nice. He's just introverted. He daydreams a lot. He likes stories and writing. Laila, can I show her the story he was writing?"

She's getting up before Laila even finishes nodding. She goes into another room and returns with a folder, sits beside Rebecca on the couch, and opens it. "It's about this boy in Africa, trying to figure out what to do after his whole village is kidnapped by slavers."

Rebecca skims the first couple of paragraphs. "This is really well-written. Could I borrow it?" She hopes to get a chance to read all of it before the mindcast ends.

"Yes," Laila says, before Yakeera can ask her.

Yakeera hands Rebecca the folder. "You see, he's really smart and good at his schoolwork. I can't remember him ever getting into trouble. That's why none of this makes any sense."

"What about his friends? Has he made any new ones lately? Anyone who might be a bad influence?"

"We've been talking about that. We don't really know who his friends are now. You know, he's a teenager. Did you tell your parents who your friends were then?"

"Not if I could help it," Rebecca says.

"Right. So, sure, we know who he played with in elementary school, but we've got no idea who he's hanging with now."

"Is there anything else in his life that might be affecting him?"

Yakeera shoots a look at Laila, who finally speaks. "It's been hard for my boy, these last few weeks. I lost my job. Then I got hit by a car. I get these headaches… it's like someone driving a nail through your head. I have to take stuff for the pain. I haven't been there like I should for my boy. He's been taking it hard. Trying to get a job to make money for us. It's been so hard. Nothing to fall back on."

"I'm very sorry to hear about your setbacks. What kind of job was he trying to get?"

"Dog-walker and I'm not sure what else. But it's hard finding work when you're thirteen."

"So he didn't actually get a job?"

Laila shakes her head. "Least not that I know of."

Rebecca thinks for a moment. There's something here, for sure. A sensitive kid like Ethan might be frantic over his mother losing her job, becoming ill, and their having no income. He might've tried other ways of making money.

"Does he have any adults in his life, aside from the two of you? A favorite teacher, coach, or pastor?" Rebecca is thinking if there is such a person, they'll be the next one to interview.

"He likes Mr. Flannery. That's his English teacher. He helped him become a better writer. And he told me he liked the gym teacher. A new guy this year. I can't remember his name."

"Okay, good, that's helpful. Is there any adult in his life you think might be a bad influence?"

Laila gets an expression like she's fuming. "His no-good uncle."

"Oh? What's his name?"

"Ray Pitt," Yakeera says. "He lives at the tent city under the freeway." She describes how to find it after Rebecca asks for clarification.

"He talked his brother—Ethan's father—into some drug deal," Laila says, warming to her narrative. "They got caught, got prison time for it. My husband became ill and died in there. That's what they said. Wouldn't be surprised if someone stuck a knife in him and they lied about it."

"Ray served his time and got out," Yakeera says. "I don't think he's so bad. It's tough getting a job when you're an ex-con. I've seen him with Ethan. He loves the boy."

Clearly Laila doesn't agree. "Someone who broke the law is always going to be a bad influence on my boy."

"Do you think he might be responsible for taking Ethan somewhere?"

Laila shrugs. "Police said Ethan's not with him and he's just sleeping in that camp most the time."

Still, another avenue to be investigated, though Rebecca is not looking forward to visiting the homeless camp.

"Have you looked through Ethan's belongings? Did that turn up anything interesting?"

"We did," Yakeera says. "Didn't find anything that would explain his disappearance. Most interesting thing we found was that story." She nods at the folder in Rebecca's lap.

"Is there anything else you can think of that might be relevant to Ethan going missing?" Rebecca says.

After a moment's silence, the sisters look at each other, shake their heads.

Rebecca stops the recording and pockets her phone. She stands up. "Thank you. I'll be in touch if I learn anything new."

Laila's eyes fill with tears. "Let us know right away if you find out anything."

It's hard for Rebecca to restrain her own tears on leaving the house. But she straightens her spine. She knows from experience the only way to move forward is to force herself not to dwell on feelings of misery or hopelessness.

She tries to read Ethan's story inside her car but has barely begun the second chapter before the mindcast ends.

Chapter Twenty-Eight

REBECCA DID a little research to confirm the location of the homeless encampment where Ethan's Uncle Ray had been living. He isn't living there anymore because it was cleared out by local authorities.

But her focus is on the past. On the night following her mindcast to Yakeera and Laila, she jumps back to the same day again. It's helpful to know what she was doing that afternoon—hanging around her apartment until it was time to go to work. This way she doesn't accidentally land in a version of herself that's behind the wheel of a car.

She dresses down again for her visit to the tent city. Faded hoodie, jeans that have a tear in them, dirty sneakers. No makeup or purse. She almost looks homeless herself. To complete the façade, she arrives by bus. Seems safer than parking in or walking through a sketch part of town.

It isn't possible to miss her destination, a messy array of color and grime looming ahead of her. She has to admit, homeless people make her uncomfortable, maybe because some are aggressive panhandlers, and others just sound batshit crazy. They need help, obviously. Food, housing, and healthcare, *dammit*. America. The richest country in the world and you have to pay for healthcare.

Dozens of people are here. Many lie wrapped in sleeping bags, or even just garbage bags. A woman in a wheelchair who has a streak of purple in her white hair is petting a stuffed poodle in her lap. She glances up at Rebecca approaching and calls out to her. "Hey, you're new here."

Rebecca usually avoids talking to the homeless, a policy that suddenly strikes her as cruel and elitist. "That's right," she says to the woman, who has strips of cloth wrapped around her hands and wrists. Whether it's to bandage them or keep them warm, Rebecca can't tell.

"What's your name?"

"Rebecca."

"I'm Martha." She smiles, revealing a missing eyetooth on the left. She rocks in her wheelchair. "I think we're full up here. You should go to the other one."

"Thank you, but I need to be here."

"You should go, you should go." She gets agitated. "It's too crowded, too many people."

"I'm looking for someone. Ray Pitt. Do you know him?"

"He's a Ray of sunshine. Cray-cray, ray-ray." She repeats this a few more times and ends it with a hefty, uncovered sneeze.

Rebecca's hand goes instinctively to her face, and for a second, she's horrified at not having a mask on. She calms down when she remembers this is pre-Covid.

"Do you know where he is?" she says.

"That way." Martha points. "He lives that way. Watch your step."

"Thanks." Rebecca isn't sure if she's warning her to avoid

soiling her feet with garbage or if she doesn't want her to tromp accidentally on some poor soul passed out on the ground. Either way, it's good advice.

As she continues through the camp, she wishes she had money or food to offer. But she didn't dare bring anything, afraid that if she gave something away, others would notice and overwhelm her trying to get a share for themselves.

Before long she spots a thin black man folded into a beach chair, scribbling into a notebook in his lap. It could be Ray; Yakeera said he enjoyed writing. Rebecca approaches and says his name.

When he doesn't look up, she wonders if this is some other writer in the group. But after she repeats his name louder, he squints up at her.

"Are you Ray? Ethan's uncle?" she says.

This gets his interest. "My boy. Has he turned up?"

She shakes her head. "I'm sorry. Do you mind if I ask you some questions about him?"

"Who are you?"

"My name is Rebecca Danser."

"Social worker?"

She nods. It seems easier than going into the whole writer ruse. "I'm trying to help find him. Like, trace his movements up to the day he went missing. When was the last time you saw him?"

"Police asked me this, and I said the same thing. He was here a couple weeks ago and I brought him to the pickup spot. You know, where contractors find guys to dig holes and stuff. The kid was worried about making money. I told him he could come, but they probably wouldn't take him. And they didn't."

"Did he go home after that?"

"I guess. I got picked, and I had to leave him there. I didn't think he was in any danger. The kid's been around these streets for a while. He knows how to handle himself."

That he's missing seems to contradict that, in Rebecca's mind. "Did he talk about what he might do if he didn't get picked? Like, other ways he might earn money?"

"He said something about walking dogs. I think his teacher recommended that."

Next stop, teacher.

"His teachers always like him. You know how smart he is?"

"I think so. I read some writing of his. It was amazing."

"Gets it from me." He raises the notebook and displays his tiny scrawl. "I've been writing since I was behind bars. I took classes there. I know all about it. Three-act structure, hero's journey, turning points… I taught Ethan how to write fiction."

"That's awesome. I hope you can get your work published."

He laughs. "Who's going to read stories by some ex-con homeless dude? Still, I can't help myself. They fill my head and I have to get them on paper."

"What are your thoughts on what happened to Ethan?" she says.

He taps his pencil. "I been thinking a lot about it. If anything happens to that boy, I don't know what I'll… I love him like my own son."

Rebecca waits to see if the answer is coming.

"I'll tell you what Martha thinks. I don't like my mind to go there, but… she said she's seen a guy lurking around the camp lately. Handsome black dude. I saw him once, a few days ago."

"What about him?"

"She says he looks at the boys… the young teenagers. We got a few of those around here, with their mothers mostly."

Rebecca feels a sickening sensation growing inside her at where the conversation is leading.

"She thinks he's a pedo… or maybe worse, maybe a child trafficker. Looking for kids to snatch and then maybe sell overseas. I heard about that before. Those are some sick fucks."

Wow. This feels like her first real lead. "Do you know the guy's name?"

"Nope. Don't know anything about him. I just seen him once. Hard to miss because he didn't look homeless. Nice clothes, and he smelled good. Not like anyone you normally see around here."

"Can you describe him for me? Other than he's good looking."

"Taller than him…" he nods at a young man with unfocused eyes and matted hair passing nearby. "Pumped like he works out. Not bald, but close-cut."

"Any tats or piercings?"

He considers this. "Not that I could see. But I think he had on long sleeves."

It's frustrating not to have something specific. "Anything else you want to tell me?"

He shakes his head. "Wish to god there was." He reaches out and grasps her hand. "If it's in your power, bring back that dear boy."

It's almost as if he senses she has a secret power that can help.

Leaving, she winds her way back to Martha. "Ray told me about the guy who might be a pedophile. Did you notice anything special about him, like tattoos or piercings?"

Martha shakes her head and shrinks into herself, peering around in case the guy might be watching. "No tats, hats," she whispers, "but he's a Brit Brit. Wore a Liverpoolian jacket. And he smells like crumpets."

Chapter Twenty-Nine

2019 - MINDCAST

REBECCA'S next mindcast brings her back to Ethan's school following his disappearance. Speaking to the principal first, she gives her story about being a journalist and asks who might know Ethan the best. Without hesitation, the principal refers her to Mr. Flannery, Ethan's English teacher.

She finds him alone in his classroom working on a crossword puzzle. When she asks to speak with him, he looks disconcerted to have been caught doing something for his own amusement during school hours. "Need to keep the brain sharp," he mumbles, sliding the paper to one side. "Remind me. Whose parent are you?"

At twenty-six, she doesn't expect to be mistaken for a parent of a thirteen-year-old. She guesses she could be a step-parent, though. The sudden thought of being someone's trophy wife amuses her. "No. I'm an investigative journalist." As soon as the lie emerges, she wishes she had come up with a different story. Mr. Flannery, being an English teacher, might be curious to find out more about her supposed career as a writer.

Fortunately, he displays a complete lack of interest. "I don't understand," he says.

"I'd like to speak to you about Ethan Pitt. The boy who went missing last week."

He straightens his black-rimmed glasses and scrutinizes her. "I'm sorry. Are you from the police?"

"No, I'm a journalist."

"I see. From the Chronicle?"

"I'm freelance. I took an interest in Ethan's story. I plan to write an article."

He still looks baffled. "Ethan's a gifted child. But an article? What would you put in it?"

"That's what I'm trying to figure out. I was wondering if you have any thoughts on where he might have gone, or what might have happened to him."

"I have no idea. He's an exceptional student. A fine writer. Smart. But there are negative influences in this community that sometimes affect our children."

"Is there anything specific you know about?"

"Of course not. He's not going to confide in his English teacher. But if I were to take a guess, I'd say, he may have gotten himself into trouble and doesn't know how to deal with it."

"So you think he ran away? Is that what you're saying?"

"It's certainly a possibility."

"Is there something he said that would make you come to this conclusion?"

"No. I told you. I try my best to get the kids to open up with me, but you know… middle school. An age where every child begins to reject authority. A time when kids are only focused on what other kids think of them. It's a tough time for them. Some can't deal with it."

"You don't think he might have taken his own life, do you?"

He spreads his hands wide on the desk, looking down at them. "I sincerely hope not. There's nothing more tragic than a child committing suicide. But I'm not a psychologist. Have you spoken to his family? Maybe he was seeing a therapist? I'm sure they would have much more insight on the issue than I would."

"Let me ask you this," Rebecca says. "Last week, when he was in class, did you notice anything different about him? Did he seem quieter than usual? Did he seem sad, or out of sorts? Any changes in his behavior that you noticed?"

"Miss, have you ever tried teaching a classroom full of unruly pre-teens? There isn't any time to observe nuances of behavior on a daily basis. From what I recall, he seemed normal. But I couldn't possibly say for certain."

"He went missing on the Saturday. Is there any chance he tried to contact you that day?"

"I was away for the weekend. I have a favorite camping and fishing spot up north, and I go there frequently. So, no, I didn't hear from him."

She stifles her frustration. After all, she could not have expected to learn much from Ethan's teachers. "Is there anything you can tell me that might shed light on what happened to him?"

He pauses, thinking. "Ethan is a very imaginative boy. I told you he's a talented writer. He's also an excellent story-teller. He might've wandered off on an adventure of his own imagining. If he does return… and I very much believe he will… he'll probably weave an excellent tale regarding what happened to him during the time he was gone."

If she hadn't come from the future… if she didn't know

that he has now been missing more than a year with no sign of his ever returning... she might almost have been convinced by Mr. Flannery's optimism. No one wants to think the worst has happened to a child.

"Thank you." She rises and glances out the window at a striking black man passing by.

"Would you like to leave your card? In case I think of anything helpful?" Mr. Flannery says.

She has no cards and since she will be ending this mind-cast soon, she also has no need of his ever calling her. She looks inside her purse like they must be in there. "Sorry. I guess I ran out. Can I drop it by the office for you later?"

"Sure."

She still has her eyes on the man outside when he turns toward the front of the school. The name "Liverpool" is printed on the right side of his jacket. The *Liverpoolian*, as Martha called the handsome creepy guy who had been hanging around the homeless camp.

"Who is that man?" Rebecca says.

Mr. Flannery follows her gaze. "Lou Johnson. The new P.E. teacher."

"New?"

"As of a few months ago."

"Nice guy?" she says.

"I don't know him very well." Mr. Flannery draws a stack of papers in front of him. "If you don't mind..."

She is already on her way, hoping to catch Mr. Johnson.

REBECCA CATCHES UP to the new P.E. teacher just as he enters the patchy school field where a handful of boys are currently running laps.

She calls out to him, but when he turns to her, he isn't smiling.

"Mr. Johnson, can I speak with you? I'd like to ask you some questions about Ethan Pitt."

"Who are you?" in clipped British tones.

"Rebecca Danser."

With reluctance, he shakes the hand she thrusts at him. His firm grasp along with the enticing vanilla scent surrounding him sets her insides aflutter, to her annoyance. For god's sake, shouldn't a gym teacher reek of sweat? But she remembers Martha saying he smelled like cake or something.

"I'm writing an article about missing children," she says. The scope of the article has expanded, now that she doesn't seem to be gathering much information about Ethan.

"I'm busy." He turns back to the kids.

"Please, Mr. Johnson. I'm trying to help Ethan and others like him."

"Are you? Or are you trying to capitalize on the trend toward diversity in publishing?"

"I'm not, but even if I were, my article could still potentially help him."

"What you write to sell an article might not be the same focus as if you're hoping to bring him home."

"You think he might have run away?"

"Actually, I don't think so. He struck me as a serious young man. I don't think he would do that. I'm very concerned that he's come to harm."

"Do you have any idea who would have a motive to hurt him?"

"No. I have to get back to my job."

"Mr. Flannery said you started working here a few months ago. Where were you before then?"

His expression hardens. "I thought you were writing about Ethan."

"Yes, but I need to get background regarding anyone who has touched his life. It would help to know if you're local to our area, or come from afar, like say…" Her eyes sweep over the word, *Liverpool*. "Like, say, the U.K."

"Do you have permission to be on the school grounds?"

"Yes, I checked in with the front office first."

"They should have told you not to disturb teachers at work." He steps away from her.

"Have you ever been to that homeless camp that's over by the freeway underpass?" she says.

His face turns explosive. "Not all black people live in poverty."

"What? No. I wasn't making an assumption. Someone there said they saw a man matching your description. I was just wondering why you would be there. Was it anything to do with Ethan?"

He tightens his lips and walks away. While she watches, he empties the ball bag and kicks the soccer balls out into the field. The kids retrieve them and start organizing for drills.

Rebecca knows she isn't going to get any more of a response out of him. But his silence speaks volumes.

The first thing she will do at the end of the mindcast is Google him and find out where he came from. If he was at another school, did something happen to any of the boys there? Why did he start a new job in the middle of the school year? And why is he so opposed to answering her questions?

Chapter Thirty

2020 - PRESENT

REBECCA WAKES bleary-eyed in the morning and decides she needs a day off from mindcasting. As much as she tries to stay in good health by walking a lot and eating oversized meals whenever she's in real-time, her nightly travels take a toll.

She steps on the scale and discovers she's down two pounds. It's part of a general trend; she's lost seven pounds since she began hunting for Ethan. She isn't too upset, however, since she's been meaning to shed five pounds since last year. *The Time Travel Diet*, she thinks. If everyone could mindcast, she would make a fortune on the book.

It would be funny if a lot of other people had gotten sparked by similar rocks that maybe landed in a meteor shower or were sprinkled over the earth by aliens. What if every other person who passed her in the street was also a time traveler? And all of them too frightened to talk about it, so they would never know that many others shared their skill. Maybe during a mindcast someday, someone would turn to her abruptly, give her a knowing look, and say, *so, um, what year are you from?*

She makes herself an English muffin with peach jam and peanut butter before showering. It's a weekday, meaning it's a good time to go visit Ethan's middle school.

She stops at the office first to get permission to talk to the teachers regarding her bullshit article about the boy.

"Where can I find the P.E. teacher?" she says, wondering if he would even have an office.

Apparently he does, and they give her directions. When she knocks on the door, a female voice replies from inside. "Come in."

Rebecca finds a buff woman of about her own age seated behind the desk, dressed like she's ready to work out. "Is Mr. Johnson here?"

At first the woman appears confused, then her expression clears. "Oh, you mean the last P.E. instructor. He left at the end of the school year."

Now it's Rebecca's turn to be baffled. "He left? After only half a year?"

"I'm his replacement."

"Was there a problem? Isn't that unusual for a teacher to leave a post so quickly?"

"Sorry. I'm just the new guy. No one told me why he left."

"Did he get fired?"

"I don't know."

It's clear she's not going to get any information here. Rebecca returns to the office and asks to speak to the principal. "I was hoping to talk to Mr. Johnson. I heard he was close to Ethan, the boy who went missing."

"Was he? I don't know. But I'm afraid he no longer works for us."

"Do you know why he left?"

"He told us it was because of a family emergency. His mother, I think. She became ill, and he wanted to move near her, to help care for her. In another state."

"Which state?"

"Hmm, I can't remember."

"Did he leave a forwarding address?"

"I don't know. You can check with my assistant."

"Overall, were you happy with his performance? There wasn't any problem?"

"Oh no. The boys liked him. Maybe the staff not so much, though."

"Oh?"

"Nothing specific. It's just, he wasn't very friendly. Didn't like to talk about himself. I don't believe he made any friends."

"I see. Well, thanks for your help."

She checks with the assistant on her way out, but there is no forwarding address to be found, nor does the assistant remember what state he claimed his ailing mother lived in.

When she gets home, she goes straight to her computer and launches a search on him. But the only thing that comes up is a brief mention of a soccer match won by the middle school team, coached by Johnson.

She checks social media too, and still can't find him. He has a frustratingly generic name, which makes it even more difficult to pinpoint this particular Lou Johnson. At the end of two hours, she leans back from the screen, her spine tingling.

A secretive man who has access to boys, and one of them goes missing. And then the man goes missing.

It has to be him. Despite her previous resolution to skip

mindcasting tonight, she decides she can't put it off. She'll take a nap, eat a healthy dinner, and then nail this guy. Somehow.

Ethan

Chapter Thirty-One

ALL WEEK LONG, Ethan tries not to think about the stealing he did with Teshi and Antoine. But when he's outside, and a cop passes near him, he keeps his face turned away. What if they have a photo of him from a security camera and are looking for him right now? It makes him frightened to leave the house and be seen by anyone.

He only goes where he has to go, meaning school, and then right back home. Ma continues in a bad state and he has to take care of her. He shops and does the laundry and prepares their food and cleans up after. The money is running out, and he wants to try getting a real job, but he doesn't have any time to even look for one.

He hopes to never see Antoine again. Teshi is in his English class, but she runs off when the bell rings. He hasn't spoken to her since the night they were together and she kissed him. He's not sure what's up with her. After the kiss, he thought maybe she wanted to be his girlfriend, but now it seems like she's avoiding him.

It's Saturday afternoon when a call comes in from her. At

first, his stomach flutters, but cold reality dampens his excitement. What if she's calling because Antoine wants them to steal again? Before he can decide whether to answer, the ringing stops.

Dude, where are you? Teshi texts.

Ethan rubs his wristband nervously. He can't just run away from this. Antoine has his picture committing a crime. The man threatened to turn him in if he didn't do his bidding. Would he really? Wouldn't he worry Ethan would then do the same to him? Maybe not. After all, chances are good Ethan doesn't know his real name, and he definitely doesn't know where to find him. Even if they did somehow pick up Antoine based on Ethan's description, there's nothing to prove the old man committed a crime, aside from Ethan saying so. Ethan is the actual person who committed the crime, and there's at least one photo that proves it.

With a sinking heart, he realizes he can't just blow Antoine off. But maybe this call from Teshi isn't about him. Maybe it's about her wanting to hang out with Ethan. He has to take a chance and respond. *Home,* he texts back.

She texts him to meet her at a specific street corner in ten minutes.

What are we gonna do? Ethan texts.

Antoines gonna take us for a drive.

Exactly what Ethan was afraid of.

Stop worrying. It's like she reads his mind. *Were not doing a job today.*

What are we doing?

You'll see. Nothing bad. She includes a kiss emoji at the end.

He hurries to get ready and checks in on Ma before leaving. Since reading now gives her a headache, she's watching TV again, and looking more alert than she has in a while. He makes up a lie about going to see a friend. He doesn't want to get *oh, is she your new girlfriend* comments if he mentions Teshi.

She's at the corner when he arrives, wearing her sexy new jacket, dope shoes, and slim pants. Her face brightens when she sees him. "Hey, it's cool. Don't look so worried, Ethan."

"Don't you think he's gonna want us to do something?"

"No, dude, I told you. This is what he calls a practice session. Shows us how to get better. Last thing he wants is for us to get caught."

Ethan believes at least that much is true. Before they can talk more, Antoine's car pulls up and they hop in, with Teshi keeping her spot in the front. Antoine greets her then turns to look at Ethan. "Hey, nice to see you. Thanks for coming."

"You're welcome," Ethan mumbles.

Antoine turns on the rap music on his playlist, signaling he doesn't want conversation right now. They drive to a storage facility on the outskirts of town and follow Antoine into a large unit with boxes stacked on the sides, but empty through the middle. He rolls down the door with them inside. Though he leaves it open a few inches on the bottom, the place makes Ethan claustrophobic, wondering if they'll get enough air.

"Show him," Antoine says, turning his back on the kids.

Teshi approaches him quietly, slips her fingers into his back pocket, and pulls out his cell phone.

"Not bad," he says. "Quicker next time. Let's show Ethan his part."

"Come here," Teshi says to him. "You're going to be walking up to Antoine and bumping into him. Pretend it was an accident. Apologize but act annoyed too. Here, I'll show you."

She approaches Antoine, trips, and falls into him, banging his arm.

"Hey!" Antoine says. "Watch where you're going."

"Sorry! But dude, you were blocking the way."

"Okay." Antoine looks at Ethan. "I want you to do that now."

He nods and positions himself against the wall across from Antoine. When the old man takes a couple steps, he moves forward and bumps into him lightly.

"Try it again. Harder. I can take it." Antoine gives his frigid smile and they start over.

This time Ethan bumps him hard, enjoying it, taking out his aggressive feelings toward him.

At the same time, just when Antoine is thrown off by the bump, Teshi is behind him, whisking the phone out of his pocket. He doesn't seem to notice.

"You see how it works, yeah?" Antoine says. "One to distract, one to take. Teshi's good at the picking part; we'll keep you as the bumper."

For about an hour, they practice the move over and over, concentrating on the best ways for Ethan to create a distraction, while Teshi works on refining her pickpocketing so that Antoine barely feels it.

"What happens if the dude realizes what we did?"

"You run," Antoine says. "But you'll be moving quickly anyway. As soon as she gets the phone or wallet, she's heading to the nearest corner, alley, or other hiding place. If it looks like the mark is onto you, don't talk to them after bumping. Just get the hell away from there as fast as you can. They can't really tie you to the theft. You accidentally collided with them; you didn't take anything."

Ethan looks at Teshi. "Have you done this before?"

She laughs. "Shit, yeah. A lot more than taking laptops from restaurants. That's riskier."

"Let's get out of here," Antoine says. After they pile out of the unit, he disappears around the corner to take a leak.

When Ethan and Teshi are alone, he says in a low voice, "You sure he's not a perv?"

"What do you mean?" she says.

"He likes having your hand in his pocket."

"Fuck you. This is business. He's a professional. He never tried to do anything pervy with me. We're all here to make money, that's it."

"A professional? He's an old dude getting kids to do his dirty work."

"I'm telling you, don't talk smack about him. I'm doing this because I like doing it. I can quit any time I want, but I won't, because there's nothing better than looking back at the mark and seeing that expression of panic on his face when he realizes you've swiped his fucking phone."

Sometimes he really doesn't know what to think about her. She says shit like this and sounds like an awful person. But at other times she's sweet, even vulnerable.

Antoine comes back around the corner and they all gather into the car. Ethan is feeling better about this so-called job. The pickpocketing seems easier than what they did before. More likely they can get away with it. They can choose their spots, making sure there aren't cameras around on the street. He had never planned on making money as a thief, but he's desperate. And Teshi makes it seem almost normal.

Chapter Thirty-Two

OVER THE LAST WEEK, Ethan has gone on pickpocketing expeditions three times. He's getting faster and more adept at his job of distracting the mark. The first time he screwed up, and they had to run away. The next two times they were well out of the area before the marks realized anything was missing. They got a cell phone once, and a wallet the next time. They turned it all over to Antoine and he paid them twenty dollars each for every successful hit.

He doesn't like what he's doing. He isn't proud of himself. But he's thinking he could live with it. If he's careful, he won't get caught. And Teshi's arguments, that life hasn't been fair to them… that rich whities get everything and black people don't get shit… are starting to make sense to him. It's not his fault his parents couldn't provide a good living for their family. Shit, it wasn't their fault either. When has a black person ever gotten a fair shake in America?

Antoine has another routine he likes. It's called driving around in his car looking for crimes of opportunity. Sometimes it's as easy as grabbing stuff from people's yards. More often, to get anything worth swiping, they have to find garage doors left open with no one watching. It has to be a house close to the curb, so Antoine can idle the car in front of the driveway, and Ethan or Teshi can dash out and snatch the first valuable thing before darting back.

Since Ethan joined them, they've nabbed a toolbox, a new pair of shoes, and the biggest prize—a snowboard. All without being spotted by anyone.

So that's what they're doing this Saturday afternoon, with Teshi riding shotgun, and Ethan in the back as usual.

"There's one." Ethan, leaning forward, is the first to spy an open garage up ahead. Antoine slows down as he nears it.

"There's a laptop on the workbench." Teshi's voice quivers with excitement.

Sure enough, the computer is open like someone's just been using it. Since no one is around, they must've popped inside for something.

"Teshi, you get it," Antoine says.

Ethan figures he picked her because she's faster and more experienced. A laptop is a prize you don't want to risk losing.

She's already wearing the big hoodie they keep in the car for jobs like this. She covers her head and face pretty well before getting out and glancing around. Seeing no one in the vicinity, she sprints to the garage and snatches the device.

"Hey!" A big man barrels through the door from the house.

Teshi doesn't pause or turn around, just keeps on moving. But this guy is fast, despite his size. "Gimme that!" He catches Teshi by the arm and spins her around. She swings the laptop and hits the man in the shoulder with it.

It's not too hard of a hit, but now he's furious. "You little shit!" He grips her on both sides and flings her back toward the garage. The computer flies out of her hands, and her head smashes hard against a concrete pillar, with the sound of a sickening thud.

Ethan watches this scene play out with dread growing inside him. *Fuck, fuck, fuck.*

Antoine pulls out into the street and they screech away from there. Resigning Teshi to her fate.

"You can't leave her!" Ethan cries out.

"Fuck I can't."

"She's hurt!"

"They'll take her to the hospital. She'll be fine."

"They'll arrest her!"

"And send her to juvey. She'll be out in no time."

Ethan shouldn't be surprised. He ought to know by now what a callous motherfucker Antoine is.

The old man says nothing during the drive back to the hood. He leaves Ethan two miles from his house, and the boy must drag his feet the rest of the way. To his surprise, Ma is in the kitchen, making homemade mac and cheese for them. "I'm feeling better today," she says. "Sit down and have some of this delicious pasta."

His stomach feels like he swallowed a brick already, but he forces down a few bites.

"What's wrong, baby?" Ma says.

"Not feeling so good."

She presses her wrist against his forehead. "I don't think you have a fever."

"It's my stomach."

"Maybe it's something you ate. What did you have for lunch?"

"I don't know. I just wanna lie down and watch some TV." He turns it on and stretches out on the couch. But he has no clue what he's watching, while the image of Teshi getting battered like a rag doll plays over and over in his head.

Ma manages to clean up and then goes to her own room. But later, after he's changed into his pajamas, gotten under the covers, and turned out his light, she comes in and sits in the chair by his bed. Her voice so soft and tender swirls over him:

Sing to me, sing to me, sing to me
Lullaby, lullaby, lullaby
Of the leaves.
He weeps with his face turned to the wall.

Chapter Thirty-Three

THE DAY AFTER THE ASSAULT, Teshi's mother calls Ma in hysterics and tells her that her daughter is in a coma and no one knows if she'll ever come out of it. Then on Monday, Mr. Flannery announces it to the class.

In the hallways, among the kids, everybody is talking about what happened. At least, what is known about what happened. How Teshi had been stealing from somebody's house, and then she got beat up, and that's how she ended in a coma. How she'll be in deep shit if she recovers, because the cops want to arrest her and maybe even charge her as an adult for attempted burglary of an expensive item. Ethan hadn't known until now that more valuable items count as felonies, and if the crime was a felony, they can choose to prosecute her as an adult.

At first everyone defends Teshi. Some kids assume she was beaten up by the cops because she's black and that's just what they do. Police over-reach. But then it comes out she was attacked by the homeowner. Somebody gets a picture of the man and everybody sees he's white. So again, all the kids are pissed that a white man was allowed to nearly kill a black girl just because she tried to take something of his. *Why isn't anybody arresting him*, they all ask. Teshi's crime was nothing compared to someone beating a kid so bad she ended up in a coma.

But apparently, it's allowed for people to defend themselves and their property when anyone trespasses. It's even allowed to shoot and kill a person who does that. But Ethan knows it doesn't work that way for black folk. If someone broke into Ethan's apartment, and his mother shot the man dead, you could be sure the police would show up right after and do the same to both Ethan and Ma. Especially if the intruder was white.

Ethan feels numb, almost like he's looking at himself from outside, making the motions of going through his day. He's in a daze, unable to concentrate on anything, let alone his schoolwork. When Mr. Flannery calls on him, he has no idea what the question was, or what his teacher had been talking about for the last ten minutes. But Mr. Flannery knows the kids are upset over the news about Teshi, and doesn't insist on an answer.

By the time Ethan reaches P.E. class, his last of the day, he's feeling at the end of his rope. Changing into his gym clothes, he overhears Jonas and Noah talking.

"Can you believe that about Teshi?" Noah says.

"Dude had no right to mess her up like that," Jonas says.

"What's she doing stealing his shit, though?"

"She's always been like that. One time I saw her swipe Vanessa's bracelet right off her desk when she turned away for two seconds."

"True dat. Nobody spent more time in the principal's office than her."

"That's what I'm sayin'. Girl had it coming to her," Jonas says.

The heat has been growing inside Ethan during this conversation, and finally, at these words of Jonas, he spins around to face him, grabs him by the arms, and slams him against the lockers.

"What the fuck, man?" Jonas shoves Ethan back.

"Hey, hands off each other!" Mr. Johnson comes around the corner.

"He started it," Jonas says.

"That true?" Mr. Johnson says.

Ethan stares at the floor.

"Go out to the field. I want everyone doing their laps." Mr. Johnson looks at Ethan. "Not you."

The other boys file out of the locker room. Mr. Johnson sits on the bench beside Ethan. "You and Teshi were friends, weren't you?"

He nods.

"Really sorry to hear what happened to her."

"Me too."

"You know what she's accused of doing, right?"

"Doesn't matter, nobody's got a right to hurt a kid like that." Ethan feels his head grow hot again.

"Calm down. I agree with you. But I need to ask… do you have anything to do with what Teshi has been up to?"

A chill sneaks down Ethan's spine. He hadn't expected anyone to make the connection. "No," he says. *Of course not. What kind of idiot would admit to that?*

Lou stares at him like he doesn't believe it. "I'm not asking to get you into any sort of trouble. I'm not the police. If you're in over your head, you can talk to me. Maybe I can help." He takes his phone out of his back pocket. "What's your cell?"

Ethan is about to tell him when he realizes he can't do that. It's supposed to be a burner. It's tied up in his criminal activities. Probably has texting evidence against Teshi, and himself. "I broke it." He prays Lou doesn't look in his locker, where it's in the pocket of his jeans.

"That sucks." Lou takes out the little notepad and pencil he keeps in his shirt pocket and scribbles down a phone number. "This is my personal number. If you need help, or just someone to talk to, borrow a phone from somebody and call me. Anytime. Anywhere. Got it?"

He nods, taking the paper handed to him. "Okay," he mutters.

"Get dressed and go home. You're excused from P.E. today."

"Thanks, Mr. Johnson."

His teacher leaves him alone in the locker room. Ethan gets out his clothes and starts changing back. He's never had a teacher like Mr. Johnson before. *Anytime? Anywhere?* Aren't there rules about not seeing kids outside of school? On the one hand, he desperately needs an honest adult he can confide in. On the other, he's learning not to trust anyone, especially those who pretend to want to help you.

Chapter Thirty-Four

STRANGELY, Ethan has never visited anyone in the hospital before. Even his mother after the car accident.

Apparently, you can just waltz right in and look around. But because he doesn't know where to go, he stops to ask at an information desk. They give him instructions to take the elevator to the third floor. Once there, he asks again at the nurse's station, and they direct him to Teshi's room.

Seeing her brings a sudden tightness to his chest. He forgets to breathe while he takes in all the machinery around her and attached to her, almost like she's part of it. A robo-girl.

She looks bad. Real bad. Her eyes are closed, her cheeks hollow, her skin wan. A bandage is wrapped around her head. She has stitches on her right arm and hand.

He can't turn his eyes away from the train wreck that is Teshi.

"Ethan," a woman says.

Only then does he realize Teshi's mother is in the room

with them. Seated in the corner with yarn and knitting needles in her lap.

She pats her face with a tissue. "My little girl, Ethan. Look what's happened to my little girl."

"She'll get better, won't she?" he says.

Teshi's mother has no answer.

"I'm sorry." If ever an apology sounded inadequate to his ears, it is now. He should never have gone along with the stealing. He should've tried to convince her to give it up. She liked him. Maybe she would've listened to him.

"It's my fault," her mother says. "I been so busy. I should've known something was wrong. She told me she had a real job. It was a lie. I should've known. I should've checked on her."

Ethan doesn't know what to say. Her remorse is too much for him. He wishes he hadn't come. Some misplaced sense of loyalty. There's nothing he can do here. No way for him to help.

She sets aside her knitting, rises and grasps his arm. "Pray with me."

The room is suffocating him. He needs to get out of there as fast as possible. He can't stand looking at what happened to her a second longer.

But a nurse sticks her head in and smiles at him. "Are you her brother?" she says.

"Her friend."

"Nice of you to come visit."

"He's going to pray with me," Teshi's mother says.

He's trapped, with the nurse blocking the door.

"Come here beside me." She draws him to the corner of the room.

"I'll get another chair," the nice nurse says.

He leans against the wall, feeling dizzy. When the chair comes, he sits next to Teshi's mother, and she takes his hands in hers. "Lord Jesus Christ, by your patience in suffering…," she starts. Ethan doesn't know any prayers, except the one he would say with his mother at bedtime, but he closes his eyes and repeats, "my Lord and my God, amen," when prompted by Teshi's mother.

Afterward, she releases his hands, and he opens his eyes wishing for a miracle, but Teshi looks no different than before. What good are prayers if they never work? What good is a god who doesn't make your prayers come true? Ethan knows it's blasphemy to think this way, but he can't help himself. He prayed many times a day when his father became ill in prison. Then his father died.

Teshi looks like she's going to die too.

"You can talk to her," Teshi's mother says. "They say people in a coma can hear you. They say it soothes them."

Ethan approaches the bed. *What the hell am I going to say to her?* She wasn't his girlfriend. They were barely friends at all the last few years. "Um, I hope you get better soon, Teshi," he says.

"Hold her hand," her mother says. "Tell me if she moves her fingers."

He wishes he hadn't come. He hasn't ever held her hand before, and now is a weird time to start. "I have to go." He rushes out before her mother can protest.

"Come back tomorrow," he hears her say as he races to the elevator. He's not coming back tomorrow. He's not sure if he'll ever come back. He knows he's being a coward, but it doesn't change how he feels.

On the bus on his way home, his phone buzzes. A call

from Antoine. It twists his stomach, thinking what that man did to Teshi. He doesn't answer.

The text comes after the phone stops ringing. *The pizza is here*, the message says. It's a code that means, *come to our meeting place asap*.

But he's already decided he isn't going. He's never going near Antoine again, if he can help it. He's going home, and he's going to lock the door, and maybe even pull the heaviest chair in front of it. He'll keep his phone next to him and call 9-1-1 if it comes to that. From now on, he'll be watching his back, and going nowhere except school and then directly home. Their money will run out soon, and if that means they'll be homeless, so be it. They'll live next to Uncle Ray and he'll watch out for them. He'll take care of Ma best he can.

It isn't till Ethan gets home and starts making dinner that one more text arrives from Antoine. *Last chance for pizza. Or else.*

Whether Antoine means he is planning to hurt Ethan, or that he's planning to turn him in to the police using the picture he took of him stealing the laptop, makes no difference. His life is over.

Amari

Chapter Thirty-Five

AMARI TELLS *Panya about his family and his village and his quest to save them.*

"I will help you," she says.

"It is going to be hard."

"I am used to hardship. I lost my parents when I was seven and have survived on my own since then. Which way should we go?"

"The slavers will take them to their ships to carry them across the ocean. We must continue west to the water."

They walk for three days until their supplies are nearly gone.

"Maybe we can find work in the next village to pay for what we need."

"There is no time for that," Panya says. "We must steal. It is not fair that they have everything and we have nothing, especially since we are trying to save your village."

He does not argue because he knows stealing will be the quickest way, and they cannot afford to delay any longer. The ships could set sail any day now on the coast.

When they approach the next village, they decide to sleep hidden behind trees during the day, and enter at night to steal what they need.

They wake late after all the fires in the village have been extinguished. Panya presses a finger to her lips before leading Amari. They are both barefoot and step lightly. Only animals could hear their approach.

They have each brought a sack in which to store the things they take. They have gotten lucky in that the villagers appear to be very trusting here. Dried meats, fruits, and stores of water have been left out everywhere. Amari and Panya grab as much as they can carry.

But before they are out of the village, Panya spots an item of great value... a hatchet. She knows Amari's spear was stolen, and he needs a weapon to confront the slavers. Amari is walking ahead of her and does not know she has paused. She lets him keep going, not wanting to make noise in stopping him. She tiptoes to the hatchet and snatches it up. But in doing so, her pack tips open and everything she has already taken tumbles out, making a terrible noise.

Amari hears this sound and turns back. As he watches in horror, a large man emerges from the hut holding a spear. Seeing Panya holding his hatchet and surrounded by other stolen goods, he thrusts his spear right through her. Her body falls limp.

Amari is frozen in terror, not knowing if there is any point in trying to help her. It looks like she must be dead. And now the man has seen him and ducked back into his hut. Amari has no doubt he is seeking another spear to kill him.

Amari drops his pack full of all the food and water he so desperately needs, and sprints into the darkness, running like the wind and not looking back.

Chapter Thirty-Six

AMARI RUNS FASTER *than he ever has in his life when escaping the village. He tries to wipe the image of Panya's body from his mind, but he cannot. The spear piercing her, the low cry she emitted, the slump of her slender form over the weapon… these pictures play out in his mind over and over as he flees.*

He is only vaguely aware of things around him. The shouts of the villagers, and the noise of their pursuit. The sky being lit by their torches. The sharp rocks that cut into his bare feet; the branches that scrape his arms. Even the snarl of a lioness when he passes her, lying with her cubs. She is angry but fortunately cannot be bothered to chase him.

Soon enough, the raucous sounds of the villagers lessen. The sky darkens. They have given up and gone home. Amari is not even worth killing.

Despite his hunger and thirst, he runs all night and all the next day until he comes to the coast. He sees only the irony—that at last he made it to his destination, but without any means of saving anyone. Unable even to save himself, he collapses amidst a pile of rocks at the base of a cliff, and passes out.

When he wakes again, the moon has risen. He forces himself to get up and climb the promontory. He must crawl like an animal, dragging himself forward with slashed and aching hands, balancing on swollen, blistered feet. The moon is in the other hemisphere by the time he reaches the top and stares out at the sea.

He perceives the outline of a magnificent ship, twenty times the size of any boat he has seen before. Its glorious sails billow in the wind and spirit it away from the shore. This is the slavers' ship, bearing everyone he has known and loved across the sea, never to be seen again.

He drops to the ground and weeps, but even in that, he fails. He has no more moisture for tears.

When the ship is only a tiny speck in the distance, he looks down at the jagged rocks below him. He might as well jump and avoid the slower torture of thirst and starvation. Panya's death plays out in his head again, and he feels the spear as if it was thrust into his own torso. Life is too cruel and not worth living. He might as well jump.

Rebecca

Chapter Thirty-Seven

2019 - MINDCAST

REBECCA HAS BEEN SITTING in her car outside The Blazing Horse pub for the last ten minutes, pondering her next move. Upon arriving in this time, she went to Ethan's school and waited across the street for two hours until Lou Johnson the P.E. teacher drove out of the lot. She managed to follow him back to his apartment, which was lucky since she didn't know how else she would find out where he lived. Ian Slate's P.I. services would not help her here; he had no idea who she was in 2019, and the process of rehiring him and waiting for results would take much more time than she had during a mindcast. She's typically limited to only five or six hours, because once she falls asleep, when she wakes up again, she's always back in real-time. It's a rule she learned early on—no sleeping during mindcasts.

Instead, she has to do a lot of waiting around, trying hard not to doze off. Her phone entertains her. She reads articles (not too many, or they'll put her to sleep), listens to podcasts (same issue), and plays games. She's thinking about signing up for Duolingo if mindcast surveillance becomes an ongoing part of her life. Then she can learn a new language while waiting for her quarry to make a move. But she hasn't decided which one yet.

She's getting better at tailing cars through traffic too. Or maybe it's just that it's easier during daylight hours. Though she had to wait another hour and a half outside Lou's apartment, at least it was still light when he went out in his car again. The chase electrified her at first; she thought for sure he was on his way to find Ethan. But then, to her great disappointment, he turned into this English-style pub parking lot and went inside.

She's contemplating whether she should continue to linger outside, or go in and observe him. She might see something useful, like Lou talking to a suspicious character, or making or receiving a phone call that gets him excited. Anything that might have relevance as to what comes next.

On the other hand, if she enters the pub, she risks doing something that might change the timeline. If he notices her watching him, and thinks she might be a cop, he's not going to take the chance of kidnapping anyone tonight. And then this trip back in time will be wasted.

In the end, necessity drives her inside. During four hours of surveillance, she has finished two bottles of water and desperately needs to pee. With luck, she can use the bathroom without becoming a customer, and just take a brief glance in Lou's direction while she's coming and going.

The place has a large bar section and a smaller eating area next to the windows. It's crowded, though a few empty seats remain at the counter. Probably two thirds of the clientele is male. Most eyes are on the soccer game playing on two large screens, though there are signs of boredom setting in. Midway through the second half, the score is four - nil, and even Rebecca knows the game well enough to understand it's a blowout. The losing team has virtually no chance of turning things around.

Squeezing past other customers, she spots Lou at a table with two other men. He and his friends are focused on the game. *Good.* She pushes forward toward the restrooms.

It occurs to her Lou might leave while she's occupied in the bathroom. Looking back at his table, she glimpses half a drink remaining in front of him. Unless he downs it in one gulp, she should have time.

As soon as she finishes, she confirms with a look that he's still in the pub. Relaxing a bit, she notices a girl who appears no older than six waiting outside the door. Her arms hang slack at her sides.

"Hello," Rebecca says, glancing around for the girl's mother.

The girl sniffs and wipes her nose with her hand. She passes Rebecca into the restroom and shuts the door behind her.

Rebecca continues looking for any sign of a parent. The child is young to be sent alone to the bathroom in a mostly adult venue like this one.

That's when she sees Lou looking at her. *Uh oh.* Not only looking, but when he catches her eye, he gets up from his table and walks toward her. *Should I flee?* she wonders. But it's too late, she's affected the timeline, she might as well let this play out. Besides, she's overflowing with curiosity.

He wasn't supposed to notice her, and now he looks like he's about to speak. Could he have remembered her from… when? Mindcasting can get so confusing, but she's pretty positive the only time she spoke to him was a week after today. In other words, a week after Ethan's disappearance.

She hasn't ever even spoken to him in real-time, because she can't find him in real-time. At this point, he definitely has no clue who she is.

"The girl's parents are over there," he says when he reaches her. He nods toward a couple seated in the middle of the room, engaged in a heated argument. "They didn't even notice when she walked away to use the toilet."

"You knew what I was thinking?" This image of Lou as someone concerned about children is so different than the impression she got when she first spoke to him.

"It was pretty clear from your expression.," he says.

"Poor kid."

"Yeah."

The girl emerges from the bathroom. Her eyes are red-rimmed and puffy.

"You okay, honey?" Rebecca asks.

Before the girl can answer, her mother rushes toward her, throwing dirty looks at Rebecca and Lou. "Come here, Jenna. You went to the bathroom? I was frantic when I saw you left the table." She grabs the girl's hand and pulls her back.

Rebecca and Lou exchange another look. "Should we have said something?" she says.

"Oh, I imagine she would just get defensive about her behavior. Possibly even blame Jenna for attracting the interest of two strangers. The only thing that might help is if there are friends or family members who can intervene."

"And then again, maybe it's a one-off. Can we give them the benefit of the doubt?"

He shrugs. "The way she spoke to her daughter left a lot to be desired."

The air grows thick between them as they both become aware that their conversation has grown strangely intimate.

"Liverpool or Man U?" His smile—which she realizes she hasn't witnessed until now—makes her heart rate skitter. She has entirely forgotten about the game.

"Sorry, too abrupt?" he says. "I'm a Liverpool fan myself, more's the pity."

Liverpool is the team that's nil.

"Condolences," she says. "I'm not a real fan, I just like watching the play." Better not to commit to a team because then he'll expect her to know something about it.

"Haven't seen you here before."

"No, I just… a friend told me about this place, and I was in the area, so I thought I'd pop in. First time." She decides, since she's already corrupted the timeline by drawing Lou's attention, she might as well take the opportunity to get to know him better. Does he seem like someone who could harm a child? Interestingly, he came across as far harsher the first time she met him than he does now. Maybe that change in manner came about because of guilt over whatever he might've done to Ethan.

"I was born in Liverpool," he says. "I never had a choice." He glances around.

"Where are you sitting?"

"Nowhere yet. I went straight to the bathroom. Would you like to join me at the bar?" She can't help enjoying his look of surprise at her forwardness. But he also looks pleased.

He follows her back and settles beside her.

"My treat," she says as the bartender approaches.

After they've given their orders, she jumps right into it. Mindcasting has taught her the value of time. "Do you have kids?" she says. "I'm wondering if that's what made you notice that little girl."

He gives her a sharp look, and she thinks she detects a second's hesitation before he says, "No."

If he's lying, then why?

"I teach them, though. Middle school P.E. So, yeah, I do like them. You could even say I'm trained to pay attention to them. You have any?"

She shakes her head. "Still time for that. In the meantime, I have a younger sister and little stepbrothers to contend with."

"I imagine you have lots of time." He glances at the feuding couple and their daughter, now rising from the table. The mother keeps a tight grip on her now.

"Ever wish you could save them all?" His voice is husky.

"Often," Rebecca says.

Chapter Thirty-Eight

THE MORNING AFTER HER MINDCAST, Rebecca doesn't think Lou could be the culprit. His eyes were full of compassion when he looked at that sad little girl.

She wishes she could've eliminated him entirely as a suspect by not going into the pub, following him as planned after he left, and confirming he never kidnapped the boy.

But once she decided to use the bathroom inside, it was over. And then she made it worse by not ignoring him when he tried to speak to her. Instead, she got so chummy, he asked for her phone number after she said she had to leave. This wasn't good, her flirting with a suspect. She would have to make sure it never happened again. So unprofessional. Although no one is overseeing her actions, she aims to be as professional as possible.

There had been no point in following him after that. Her presence changed the trajectory of the evening and that was the end of it.

But now she's wondering what her next step should be.

Another mindcast to the same place tonight, and this time she waits in her car? It's difficult for her to feel any enthusiasm for this plan, mainly because Lou has become an unlikely suspect in her mind. She would rather pursue a more promising lead. And if she were to be completely honest with herself, she would admit the other reason is, that the temptation to join him in the pub again might be too strong.

In the midst of her indecision, a call comes in from Yakeera. "Did you get that list I emailed you?" she says.

"I did, thanks." Rebecca has been avoiding the list of people Ethan knew, because it will require a whole new round of research.

"Well, there's one more Laila thought of. A girl, Teshi. They were friends when they were little. Her mother is a friend of my sister's. Troubled home, if you know what I mean. The dad. Laila thought she and Ethan weren't hanging out anymore, but then when Sharon called—that's Teshi's mom—when Sharon called and told her how Teshi had gone into a coma… the news upset Ethan. A lot. So, maybe they were better friends than Laila realized."

"A coma? What happened to her?"

"She got caught trying to steal something out of someone's house. The guy was brutal, smashed her head against the wall. And her just a kid."

"Poor thing. When did this happen?"

"Well, that's just it. Happened a few days before Ethan went missing. That's what got us wondering if it might be related."

It could be significant. "How's she doing?" Rebecca asks.

"She came out of the coma about a month ago. She was lucky; not many recover after so long. She's back home, still under medical care. Police want to book her, but the doctors got them to hold off a little longer. Laila spoke to her parents and they're okay with you talking to her. You want to do that?"

"Yes. Definitely." It might have no connection, but then again, it might. She gets the address from Yakeera before hanging up.

On her way over to see Teshi, she tries not to speculate too much. The girl and her stealing probably have nothing to do with Ethan. And she was in a coma for so long, she might not remember anything. Might not be coherent now at all. But it's worth investigating.

Teshi lives in a building that looks more rundown than Ethan's. A man answers the intercom and listens while Rebecca briefly explains who she is and that she got permission to come.

"I heard nothing about this," the man says. But after a pause, the door buzzes open and she lets herself in.

The apartment is on the third floor. The man, who must be Teshi's father, waits for her at the open door. He's short, with clothes that look baggy on him and a receding hairline. When he looks at Rebecca, he doesn't quite make eye contact, which, rightly or wrongly, lends him a shifty appearance.

He gives her the once over. "You're not from the police, are you? Got to tell me if so."

"I'm not, I swear it. I'm writing an article about Teshi's friend Ethan, who went missing. My questions are related to that. There won't be anything about your daughter in my article."

"I changed my mind about this. My daughter isn't well enough." He starts to shut the door.

She gets an idea. "There's payment, of course. Fifty

dollars if you let me talk to her." Lucky she stopped at the ATM on her way here. She's been making that a habit lately, because cash comes in handy now and then. Helps to have it in advance, since there won't be time to get it in the middle of whatever she's doing.

He stares at the side of her face. "A hundred."

She hesitates before nodding. He holds out his hand for the money.

"When I'm done," she says.

He hesitates again, but seems to realize he has the power to keep her there until she forks over the cash. "Okay. First door on the left. She was awake a second ago." He moves to let Rebecca pass.

She goes to the open door and looks in. Teshi is sitting, or more like slouching, in a hospital bed watching TV with the volume turned way up. She's connected to an IV.

"Hi, Teshi," Rebecca says.

The girl turns toward her, a dull look in her eyes. Rebecca's heart sinks. "May I come in?"

Her eyes brighten just a bit. "Okay."

Rebecca settles into the chair beside the bed. "Do you mind if I turn off the TV for a minute?"

Teshi nods, which Rebecca takes as a *no-I-don't-mind*. She clicks the power button on the remote. "How are you feeling?"

Teshi shrugs. "They give me drugs." She looks at the IV. "I'm not normal yet."

"Can you remember stuff from before this happened?"

"Some."

"Do you remember your friend Ethan?"

She frowns. "Course I know Ethan."

"So you were good friends? Did you hang out with him last year?"

"Sometimes."

"Cool. Can you tell me what happened the day you got this injury that put you in a coma?"

"I don't remember that part."

"They say you were trying to steal something. Do you remember wanting to do that? And don't worry, I've got nothing to do with the police."

She pouts. "Don't remember nothin' about stealing."

"I'm asking for Ethan. What you tell me might help us find him."

"Find him?"

"Yes. I mean, maybe he's still alive. I'm not giving up hope."

"What the fuck you talking about? Where's he gone?"

No one told her. *Shit.* Now Rebecca has to. "A week after you went into a coma, Ethan went missing. No one has seen him since. It's been over a year."

Her eyes widen in astonishment. Suddenly she leans forward and grips Rebecca's arm. "Antoine did it," she hisses. "Antoine must've killed him."

An electric tingle runs down Rebecca's spine. "Who's Antoine?"

Teshi's gaze shifts to the door and back. She whispers, "the old guy who made me steal."

"Is he the one who ordered you into that garage?"

She nods. "I don't really remember, but it must've been him."

"What's his last name? Where does he live?"

"I don't know."

"Was Ethan stealing for him too?"

She nods her head.

"Why would Antoine kill him?"

She shrugs. "I don't know. But maybe if Ethan said he wouldn't steal for him anymore."

"Was Ethan with you when you got hurt?"

"I don't remember. Probably."

Chapter Thirty-Nine

2019 - MINDCAST

REBECCA LEARNED where the attempted robbery took place from Teshi's father. No one, including the homeowner who assaulted her, had witnessed anyone else with Teshi, or waiting nearby. But just because no one had been seen, didn't mean they weren't there.

Having traveled back in time to witness what happened for herself, she waits in her car across the street, this time in a sleepy San Francisco neighborhood. An hour after she arrived, the man who nearly killed Teshi opened his garage door and began sawing a piece of wood, referring occasionally to instructions on his laptop. So far, he has left the computer on his workbench twice while he went into the house for several minutes at a time.

The third time he goes into the house, a gray Dodge stops abruptly in front of the driveway. Rebecca straightens in her seat, trying to get a glimpse into the vehicle, but the sun reflecting off the front windshield makes it difficult.

She gets out of her car at the same time Teshi springs from the passenger seat and runs into the garage. Rebecca's focus remains on the Dodge. She peers in at Ethan, hunched in the back seat. The man named Antoine must be the driver —a greasy, unpleasant-looking person in his sixties, she guesses. He makes her flesh crawl, the way he pimps children to carry out his crimes.

Antoine glances in her direction and is clearly unhappy to see a potential witness, but he waits for Teshi. If the home-owner hadn't returned, the girl would've been back in the car in two seconds. Tragically, the immense man with the shoulders of a linebacker charges her. Rebecca can't watch, though the sounds of the attack make her stomach roil. She tries not to listen as she notes the license plate number, repeating it inside her head. *I'm here for this.* She will use it to nail Antoine to the wall.

That cowardly motherfucker squeals his Dodge into the street and speeds off without Teshi, and with Ethan looking terrified in the back. She hauls back to her car, does a U-turn, and guns it after them. She means to track his next move and maybe find out where he lives right away, instead of waiting to see if Ian the P.I. can figure it out from his license plate number.

Rebecca manages to follow the gray Dodge all the way to Ethan's neighborhood, partly because of her initial assumption that they were headed there. Anywhere else and she likely would've lost them by now.

A mile or two from Ethan's building, Antoine jerks up to the curb and lets the boy out. Rebecca has to continue past them in order not to attract attention by stopping suddenly. In her rearview, she glimpses Ethan with hoodie pulled over his head, face lowered, and hands balled into fists. He can't get away from Antoine fast enough. She can only imagine the turmoil going on inside him.

A second later, Antoine pulls back into traffic. She waits until there's a reasonable distance between them before continuing her pursuit. It's going to be harder to tail him now that she has no idea where he might be going. Her tracking skills have improved compared to her early efforts, but even so, in her rush not to lose him, she swerves into two turns in a way that might be noticeable in his rearview. Still, he shows no signs of trying to shake her.

After five minutes of this, Antoine pulls ahead of a large truck on the right and veers onto the cross street ahead of him. Unfortunately, before Rebecca can follow, the light becomes red. The truck driver, who must be planning to continue straight, now blocks the right turn lane, forcing her to wait for the green light. Even then, there's further delay as the slow-moving truck rumbles forward.

Antoine is gone. She drives through the area for ten minutes without finding him again. At least she still has his license plate number in her head. With luck, that alone will give her the information she needs.

There's one more action she can take, though. Driving back the way they came, she parks as close as she can to Ethan's apartment. She hopes he hasn't gotten sidetracked and gone somewhere else.

Just when she's wondering if he might've reached home already, she sees him approaching along the sidewalk. His feet are dragging, and his shoulders hang low. She walks toward him, trying to make herself look as unthreatening as possible.

Deeply distracted, Ethan doesn't notice Rebecca until she moves in front of him.

"Can I talk to you?" she says.

He staggers back, nearly falling. "Who are you?"

"Rebecca Danser. I'm a social worker. I'm not with the

police or anything like that." As soon as she says it, she real-izes that was the wrong thing to say. Nothing says *I'm a cop* more than a statement like *I'm definitely not working with the police.*

"I gotta get home." He tries to get around her.

"I know you're working for Antoine."

His eyes widen. "What're you talking about?"

"You and Teshi."

"Leave me alone." His voice is thick. But when he attempts to pass her again, she grasps his sleeve.

"He's dangerous. You need to get away from him. Before he hurts you." She hopes this will reach him. He knows Teshi is already paying a terrible price for doing Antoine's bidding.

His face crumples. "What can I do?"

"Let me help you. Tell me his real name."

"I don't know it."

"Tell me where he lives, or where he meets you."

"He just drives up to street corners and picks us up. I don't know where he lives."

"Has he ever taken you somewhere?" Rebecca says.

He hesitates. "He brought us to a storage place once." He tells her the name, but it's a company that has facilities everywhere.

"What city?"

Ethan shrugs. "I wasn't paying attention."

"Why did he bring you there? He doesn't live there, does he?" She's not sure that would be possible, but it can't hurt to ask.

Ethan shakes his head and fidgets with a leather band he wears on his wrist. He describes how they practiced picking pockets while they were there.

"What else has he made you do?"

Ethan hesitates at first, but gradually opens up. The anger burning inside him over what happened to Teshi appears to be driving him. At the end, he asks, "What can you do to stop him?"

Gazing at the boy, she's reminded of Yakeera's words: *He could be your son, your grandchild, your brother. A thirteen-year-old child who disappeared. Don't you care? Doesn't anybody care?*

He deserves the truth, if only because his life may end three days from now.

"My little sister was kidnapped when I was six," Rebecca says. "I've never forgiven myself for leaving her alone. Then last year…" It was actually this year, but it's too complicated to sort out past and future at the moment. "Last year I got sparked by something and it gave me the ability to travel through time. I mean, my mind from the future comes back into my body during times in the past. So I know things that are going to happen."

Now he's staring at her like she's a crazy person.

"I actually found my sister using this ability. But it wasn't enough. When I saw your face on a poster, when I learned you were missing, I had to help you. I had to find out what happened to you."

He's no longer listening. He's written her off as a lunatic. "Hey, gotta go."

"I know you don't believe me. I wouldn't have believed me. But three days from now, remember what I said. Someone is going to try to hurt you. Protect yourself. Be safe. Don't let it happen."

"Lady, you sure you're okay?"

"You're very smart, Ethan. And kind. I read part of your story, you know. About Amari in Africa whose family is stolen by slave-traders. I hope I get to read the rest of it someday."

"Get out! Did my Ma show it to you?"

She shakes her head. "Your aunt will show it to me a year from now."

He glances around like maybe there's something to her claim of being a time traveler, and therefore the time travel machine must be nearby.

"Stay away from Antoine, and you should be safe." She knows whatever he does from now on will make no difference in real-time. But maybe it will change things for this version of Ethan. This particular thread in time, if that's what it is. "Go home. Be with your family. I'm sorry if I frightened you."

"You don't scare me," he says. "And don't worry about me. I'm not going near that son of a bitch again. It's Teshi who needs help, not me."

"She's going to be okay," Rebecca blurts. "She's going to recover."

He breaks into a smile that could light the sky. "Really?"

"Really." She can't help but smile back while he spins around and skips on his way to his apartment.

Chapter Forty

SHE'S napping in the afternoon—something she does more and more frequently since she began mindcasting so often—when the buzz of her phone wakes her. It's a text from private eye Ian Slate, who she called in the morning to ask him to trace Antoine's license plate. *Are you available to zoom now?*

Yes, she texts back. When the link arrives a moment later, she's settled into her Zooming corner.

He looks as well put-together as the last time she saw him, with his miniature teacup poised at the tip of his fingers. "Some bad news," he starts off. "The license plate is fake. Not a valid registration. We can't use it to find the owner of the car."

"Aren't you required to have a valid registration?" she says.

"Sure. But it's a misdemeanor. It's better to be ticketed for that than to take the chance of being traced while you're committing a much bigger crime. If he's smart, he's a cautious driver who doesn't give traffic cops any reason to check on his plate. If he gets caught breaking other laws, the fact that he has a fake plate will be the least of his worries."

"I see. Thanks for checking." She wonders why he didn't just text this update.

"There's more." He gives a crooked smile, and she suspects he's enjoying playing with her like this.

"Please, do tell," she plays along.

"After calling a few of my contacts in law enforcement, I managed to find one who knew someone matching Antoine's description."

When Rebecca spoke with Ian earlier, she had opened up about the case to him. There seemed no reason to keep it secret that she was trying to learn what happened to Ethan. When she reached the part where she speculated the boy might've been thieving for a scumbag named Antoine, Ian had asked for a physical description of the man, along with information about his criminal activities and methods. He didn't explain at the time how that might help.

"Oh my god. Were you able to get his name and address?"

"His name is Alex Bosko, and he was arrested about seven months ago for possession of stolen property, fencing stolen property, corrupting minors, and related crimes."

Seven months. Meaning he was still a free man at the time Ethan went missing. Still her number one suspect. "Can I go talk to him in jail?" *And try to wrench the truth out of him.*

"I'm afraid he's not there. He made bail, and then he disappeared. They can't find him."

A shiver runs through her at the thought that he might've taken Ethan with him. "What's his address?"

"You won't find him there."

"I understand, but it would help to know how close he

might've lived to Ethan. I mean, I don't really have proof this is the guy Ethan was working with." *But mostly I need the address so I can jump back in time and spy on him,* she doesn't say.

"Sorry, I didn't think you would need it at this point," Ian says. "I'll get back to you with that information."

"Thank you. You're awesome. You've been so helpful."

He shifts his gaze to something behind her. "Nice looking family. Any relation?"

Before she can answer, he has disconnected the Zoom. So much for her fake family.

Chapter Forty-One

2019 - MINDCAST

AN HOUR AFTER THEIR MEETING, Ian texted Rebecca with the home address of Alex Bosko, aka Antoine. Nothing could hold her back from mindcasting there the same night.

Since six p.m.—before Ethan has left his apartment—she has been parked down the street from Antoine's unremarkable gray house, without observing anyone coming or going. There's no way to tell if his Dodge is inside the one-car garage or not. She knows someone is in the house, though. Lights started flicking on after sunset.

She now wishes she had asked Ian to check who all was living here. A wife? A mother? *Abused children?* She needs to learn how to be more thorough, and less rushed.

Normally while surveilling a place, she keeps busy on her phone, but tonight she's too tense. She's convinced Antoine did it, he's the only one who really strikes her as a killer. Tonight she'll find out the truth, but the worst thing is, she doesn't see him as a kidnapper. A man who enlists kids to do his thieving… he's too lazy. It would be too much trouble for him to keep prisoners. He would shoot the boy and have done with it. This is the reality, and she needs to steel herself to face the atrocity she may witness.

By eleven o'clock, she can no longer stand not knowing whether it's Antoine or someone else inside the house. She checks to make certain no one is around before sneaking out of her car and silently approaching the front window. Creeping along the side, she peers through the glass and hears a late-night show on TV. However, she has to move to the next window before she's able to glimpse the small woman slouched in her chair, looking as if she has nodded off. *Must be the wife.*

Her heart leaps into her throat at the sound of an approaching vehicle. Headlights swerve around the corner. She looks around wildly for a hiding place. The car—which could be the gray Dodge—is coming this way.

She darts across the patchy lawn to the neighbor's driveway, where a mid-sized RV is parked. Just as the car is turning toward Antoine's house, she springs behind the vehicle and crouches down.

Next door, the car engine shuts off, the door opens and shuts. The car locks are beeped into place. Peering under the RV, she watches a man's feet walking toward the house. It has to be him.

Her heartbeat races. *What if Ethan's body is in the back?* It looks like a good-sized trunk, probably picked for that reason, to provide space for stashing stolen goods (and murdered children?) on the go. But more likely, Antoine would've already disposed of the poor boy somewhere. In that case, there could be evidence he plans to remove tomorrow. She needs to pop that trunk and take a look.

After she hears his front door open and close, she waits a minute longer before slinking out from behind the RV. The front lights have been shut off; chances are he woke his wife, and they went to the bedroom. There's still a glow coming from the back.

She can't wait. This mindcast has lasted longer than any other, and it could end any second now. She sprays the light from her cell phone into the car. A few items of clothing are scattered around—a hoodie, a couple of baseball caps—but nothing to indicate he's recently been out killing or digging a grave. No shovel, or blood smears on the upholstery as far as she can tell. Of course, he's not likely to leave anything incriminating outside of the trunk.

She heard him use the remote, but in case he accidentally unlocked the car instead of locking it, she tries the driver's side door. Definitely locked.

There has to be a way to pry open the trunk. She kneels so she won't be seen from the house, and tries forcing each of her own keys into the keyhole. Her smallest key at least goes into the slot. She jiggles it around, making a mental note that she needs to look up lock-picking on YouTube when she gets back. Sadly, there's no time for that now.

Then, what feels like the muzzle of a gun is pressed against her back. "Say nothing," a man hisses. "Get up and walk to the house."

She struggles for breath. How did she not hear him approaching? With her legs weak and shaking, she manages to pull herself up and move toward the open door, with him following directly behind her.

The short woman is waiting for them in the kitchen, which is dark save for the beam of a street lamp through the window. She looks downtrodden, with thin strands of gray hair framing sunken features. She wears a bathrobe over her pajamas, and fluffy slippers on her feet.

But before Rebecca can make any further observations, Antoine smacks the gun hard into the back of her skull. Crippling pain overwhelms her, then dizziness and blackened vision. She clutches her head and drops to her knees in agony.

REBECCA PRAYS that she'll pass out, ending her misery and sending her back to her own time. But she doesn't.

She's helpless while Antoine presses her flat onto the floor and holds her down. "Get the whiskey," he tells his wife.

Rebecca is vaguely aware of her scampering to a cupboard and returning with the bottle.

"Open it," Antoine says. A second later he forces Rebecca's mouth wide open and pours whiskey into her throat. Choking and coughing, she's powerless to keep from swallowing. The excess runs down her face and neck. She remembers the movie *North by Northwest*… he's trying to get her drunk… then he'll run her off a cliff.

Go back, go back, go back, she keeps telling herself in the midst of her misery. But at the very second when she thinks her mindcast may be coming to an end, a crashing noise comes from somewhere in the house, and something in her subconscious with a need to know what that is keeps her here.

Heavy steps bang across the floor. Dark hands grasp Antoine's shoulders and yank him off her. He's thrown against a metal cupboard, the whiskey bottle splintering next to him. His head must've hit the edge of it; she sees blood as he crumples down and passes out.

The slipper-covered feet skitter out of the room. A door slams and a lock turns in another part of the house.

"Are you alright?" Rebecca's rescuer says.

She blinks up at Lou Johnson, Ethan's gym teacher, and her thoughts swirl in confusion. Has he been working with Antoine? Did one of them double-cross the other? But then, if he's one of the bad guys, why save her?

She wipes her hand across her mouth, her head pulsating like someone is flogging it with a hammer. "The gun... he had a gun."

Lou looks around, spots it on the table, and pockets it. "Can you move? We need to get out of here."

Trying to raise herself causes an acute stroke of pain inside her head.

"I'll get you." He easily lifts her and carries her across the room to the front door. She sees now that he must've kicked it open. He brings her outside and lays her on the grass, helping her to sit up.

"Please," she says. "Can you get his car keys? We have to open the trunk."

"Why?"

"I'm afraid of what he might've done."

He looks ready to ask more questions, then appears to change his mind. "Do you know where they are?"

"No."

A hesitation, and then he rises and hurries back into the house. She hopes it wasn't a mistake to send him back in there. What if Antoine woke up, grabbed another gun, and is waiting to kill Lou? Or what if the meek little wife is not really so meek, and she comes out of her room with an aim to shoot her husband's attacker?

But he returns quickly, the keys jangling from his hand. He goes straight to the car and opens the back. Not being in a position to see the trunk's contents, she waits, her heart thumping as hard as the inside of her head, while he stands hidden behind the raised lid far too long.

"What's in there?" she croaks.

Lou returns to her side. "It's full of stuff he must've stolen."

Relief floods her, though at the same time, she feels confounded. *Where is Ethan?*

"Are there any signs that he hurt someone?" she says. "Blood. A shovel. Anything like that."

He shakes his head, giving her a curious look. "Who are you?"

"I'm Rebecca. A social worker. Trying to find Ethan Pitt. Now your turn."

"Ethan? He's missing?"

"Yes."

His shoulders droop. "Fuck."

"Why are *you* here?" she says.

"I've been following Antoine, or whatever the hell his name is. Hoping to catch him with the goods."

"How did you find out about him?"

"I saw him with Teshi one time. You know her? You know she's in a coma because of that beast?" He waves his head toward the house, wearing a look of revulsion.

"I heard about what was going on from some of the kids," he continues. "I'm a teacher. I listen to them, sometimes when they don't know it."

There's the sound of a siren in the distance.

"I have to go," he says. "I'd appreciate it if you just say you don't know who called them. You thought it must be one of the neighbors who heard you cry out."

"Why don't you want to talk to them?"

"I'm black." He takes out the gun and wipes it with his shirt. "You want to hang onto this?"

"God no."

He tosses it into the shrubs and before she can ask any more questions, he has disappeared into the darkness.

"Thank you," she murmurs after him.

The siren grows closer. She doesn't want to talk to them either. Not here, not now. She needs to get back to real-time. She needs to find Antoine there.

As her vision dims, signaling the end of the mindcast, the throbbing inside her head mercifully comes to an end, while the question, *where is Ethan,* reverberates.

Chapter Forty-Two

REBECCA HUNCHES BLEARY-EYED over her breakfast. What now? Has she been looking at this the wrong way?

Antoine could still very well be guilty. He might've killed and buried Ethan and destroyed the evidence before returning home. But there are some problems with that thinking. First, Lou said he was following him, and clearly he didn't witness any foul play. On the other hand, Lou could not have trailed him the entire evening, because earlier he was at the pub watching the soccer match. She wishes she had asked for more details regarding where and when he began tailing Antoine.

Second, Lou told her the trunk was full of stolen shit. Which sounds like, no room for a body. It really feels as if she's back to where she started.

She opens a new document on her computer. It helps her thought process to see things in writing sometimes. She makes a list tracking Ethan's movements the night he disappeared.

1. *6-6:30 p.m., he's home making supper.*
2. *6:30, he leaves his building in a rush, goes to Aunt Yakeera's house (observed).*
3. *6:45ish, he runs out of her house, but she calls him back and he goes to dinner with her (observed).*
4. *7:40, he gives her the slip at the restaurant, then gets in Ballard's car (observed).*

After staring at the list for a moment, she starts a new one labeled, *The Suspects.*

1. ***Antoine***, *aka Alex Bosko, is out in his car from 6:00 p.m. till 11 p.m.*
2. ***Lou Johnson*** *is at the sports bar from 7 p.m. till?? (can't be sure because I interrupted him). Sometime before 11 p.m., he tails Antoine back to his house.*
3. ***Craig Ballard*** *picks up Ethan from Dos Amigas at 7:40 p.m.. BALLARD'S CAR IS THE LAST PLACE I SAW ETHAN THAT NIGHT.*

Third list: *Conclusions.*

1. *Ballard kidnapped Ethan. He's the one who killed him or is keeping him prisoner.*
2. *Or, Ballard brought Ethan to his killer/kidnapper either knowingly or unknowingly. He knows who that person is, or saw the person and can give a description.*
3. *Or, Ballard dropped Ethan off somewhere but doesn't know who the killer/kidnapper is. Wherever he dropped him is likely to be a clue regarding the identity of the killer/kidnapper.*

Craig Ballard is the key. She needs to talk to him again, and this time she needs to be more intimidating and threatening. No more Ms. Nice Guy.

She doesn't need Ian's services this time. A quick Internet search turns up the name of the law firm Ballard works for, along with their address. Rebecca calls their office and asks to speak with him. As soon as they acknowledge he's at the office, she hangs up. It's all she needed to know.

She dresses quickly in a suit, nylons, high heels. Her hair loose and sexy. She wants to look impressive. The hotter you look, the more likely people pay attention to you. It's just the way things are. She wants the other lawyers in the office to notice her and wonder why she's there. She wants to make Ballard as uncomfortable as possible.

When she asks to see him at the reception desk, she is told he's in a meeting. She doesn't back off. "It's a family emergency," she says. "Related to a boy named Ethan Pitt, who went missing a year ago. Tell him that, please."

A few minutes later, he comes out to the lobby. He doesn't know who she is at this point; the last time she met with him was during a mindcast. He looks the opposite of pleased to see her.

"I'm Rebecca Danser," she says, rising and thrusting her hand into his. "I'm writing a story on Ethan Pitt. May we speak privately somewhere?"

"I don't know what you're talking about. Who is Ethan Pitt? If you don't leave right now, I'll have to call security."

"You know who he is. You gave him a lift outside Dos Amigas Restaurant a year ago. If you don't want to talk to me, that's fine." She lowers her voice. "I can go directly to the police, if you prefer. I have a witness stating you were the last person to be seen with Ethan before he went missing."

He lowers his volume too. "Why haven't I heard anything about this before?"

Rebecca glances toward the receptionist, who looks increasingly curious about their conversation. "Are you sure you want to talk out here?"

"Fine. Come with me." He leads her to a small conference room near the entrance and shuts the door once she's seated. "Who is this so-called witness?"

"Not saying. I'm a writer. I protect my sources." He will assume it's Yakeera. Who else might've seen him arrive at the restaurant and take off with Ethan? Rebecca hopes this doesn't put Yakeera in any kind of danger. "Look, let me lay it out for you. I don't give a shit if you were having an affair with Ethan's aunt. I'm just trying to find the boy. If you tell me what I need to know, you're not going to feature in my article. You'll be a protected source and I'll make up a name when referencing you. No one will know about your tawdry affair. You don't have to worry about this ruining your political run.

"But if you stonewall me," she says, "I'm going straight to the police, and your actions will become public knowledge. Frankly, you're going to find yourself in legal trouble as well, for not coming forward with what you knew about the case. Is that what you want? I wonder how likely you are to win the election after that? Do you want the public to know you held back valuable information because you didn't give a fuck about what happened to a black boy who's the nephew of the woman you were fucking? Is that what you want?"

He's actually starting to sweat. "Why are you doing this? What do you get out of it?"

"It might be hard for you to understand, but saving Ethan is what I get out of it. That's my goal. If a decent article comes out of it too, great. But all that is secondary to finding the boy."

He's staring down at the table. Finally, he looks up. "I did give him a ride from the restaurant. I. uh, didn't want him telling anyone about my seeing Yakeera. The kid said he needed money, so we stopped at the ATM and I got out some cash for him. A few hundred bucks. I felt bad for the kid. I think I would've given him money in any case."

"Okay. Good. Where did you take him after that?"

"At first he said he wanted to get off at a bus stop. But after I gave him the money, he changed his mind. Said he wanted to see someone instead. He didn't say who. It took a while to get there. He told me not to wait for him."

"Was it a house? An apartment?"

"They were all houses around there. But I don't believe he had me drop him too near the house he was going to. I think he didn't want me to see that."

"How do you know?"

"When he got out of the car, he walked down the street and didn't turn into any of the driveways."

"Where was this?"

Her heart sinks when he gives her the name of the town. None of her suspects live there.

Chapter Forty-Three

2020 - PRESENT

REBECCA GOES for her afternoon walk, making it longer than usual. It isn't fun breathing through a mask, but the city streets are crowded and most other people are masked, so it's a matter of consideration if nothing else. To clear her head, she tries to think about anything but Ethan. She knows that when she avoids thinking about a problem for a while, a solution sometimes magically presents itself.

She returns a few minutes before five, in time for the Zoom she has planned with Sadie. They haven't spoken for two weeks, which is the longest separation they've had to endure since Sadie was restored to her family. Her sister is like a drug with no harmful side effects to Rebecca. Just seeing her face and hearing her voice makes Rebecca giddy, and prone to spontaneous bursts of laughter.

Uncharacteristically, Sadie joins the Zoom several minutes late, just as Rebecca is about to text her a reminder. It's obvious from her expression that something is wrong.

"Tyler's missing." She huddles with her arms crossed over

her chest. Tyler is seven years old, the younger of their two stepbrothers.

Rebecca's stomach lurches. "What happened?"

"He and his brother were playing in the family room. They got into a fight over some toy, and Tyler ran off. The back door was open. Dad's looking outside. Kevin's here with me."

"Hi Rebecca." Nine-year-old Kevin greets her from somewhere offscreen. His voice is unusually subdued.

"Hold on, Marie just came home." Sadie moves away from her computer, but Rebecca can still hear her explaining what happened to their stepmother.

"Did you check everywhere?" Marie says.

"Yes, I think so." Sadie doesn't sound quite certain.

Rapid footsteps tapping against a wooden floor recede from the room, and Sadie returns to the screen. "She's checking upstairs again."

Rebecca's breathing quickens. An image flashes in her mind, her six-year-old self, trembling in the middle of a room, struggling but unable to understand the urgent questions of the police officers surrounding her.

"Have you called 9-1-1?" she manages to whisper.

Before Sadie can answer, their father speaks, his voice low and heavy. "He's nowhere outside."

"Found him!" Marie calls from upstairs. More pattering of steps.

A sensation of lightness fills Rebecca.

"Where was he?" Their dad's voice is still tight.

"He likes to read in the closet when he gets upset," Marie says.

"I thought we checked in there," Sadie says.

Tyler runs into the room and inserts his head in front of Sadie. "Hi Rebecca!" He gives her an enormous smile.

"Hey sweetie," she says. "I'm so glad you're all right. But next time you should tell someone if you're going to hide. Okay?"

"Sure." He runs off, and from the sound of it, he and his brother are soon playing happily again.

Their father appears behind Sadie and places a trembling hand on her shoulder. His face is pale. Rebecca knows exactly what he's feeling. They've been through this before, but in that case, it was the nightmare that didn't end for many years.

"Time for a glass of wine, Dad?" Rebecca asks.

He relaxes a little at the joke. "Not waiting till six, that's for sure. Hey, I wanted to ask, can you come for dinner on Saturday? Marie is making something special."

"What about Covid?"

"You've been wearing your mask, right?"

"Yeah."

"You're just one person. It's okay."

"Let me think about it. I don't want to accidentally get anyone sick." In truth, she's still not sure how she feels about spending time with them.

"Can we do our Zoom tomorrow?" Sadie says. "I think we all need time to breathe here right now."

"Of course. Everybody, relax. I'll be in touch soon."

They sign off, but Rebecca continues to stare at the screen. An idea is forming in her head. She's been concentrating so much on people who know Ethan. What if the kidnapper is someone who didn't know him? Like in Sadie's case. Or unlike Sadie's case, he might be a serial criminal. Maybe he's committed the same crime at least once before.

She texts Ian. *Can you check for any other missing boys that are similar in profile to Ethan? 11-14 years old, dark-skinned, low-income neighborhood, family not very well off. Good student? I'm not sure if that's relevant. Just in the Bay Area, for now. Last ten years?*

His response comes within minutes. *I'll get on that. Hope to have something for you tomorrow.*

Chapter Forty-Four

2020 - PRESENT

AFTER THE FIRST solid night's sleep she's had in weeks, Rebecca wakes to an email from Ian.

Five years ago in Penford, California, a twelve-year-old boy went missing. His parents are from India and they own a small Indian grocery store. Neighborhood similar to Ethan's.

Ian continues with the boy's name—*Kabir Ghosh*—followed by his parents' contact information. *Let me know if you want more names. There are several other possibilities to explore in the Bay Area, but this one was the closest match.*

Thanks and not yet, she emails back.

She quickly looks up Kabir Ghosh online. Like Ethan, he is barely mentioned in a brief local article several days after he went missing. She can find no further mention of him, aside from the listing on missingkids.org.

She decides to call the parents. It's the fastest way to find out the most she can about the case, assuming they're willing to speak with her. A woman with an Indian accent answers the phone.

"Hello, Mrs. Ghosh?" Rebecca says.

"I do not want whatever you are selling," she says.

"Please don't hang up. I'm calling about your son, Kabir."

There is a silence, during which Rebecca can imagine her jumbled feelings. Grief and fear reign on the surface, but underneath, the tiny light of hope always burns.

"Who are you?" The woman's voice is a whisper now.

"Rebecca Danser. I'm a journalist writing an article about a boy who went missing last year. I did a little research and found out about Kabir. There are some similarities between them. May I ask you some questions about your boy? It would be better to speak in person, but with Covid... I wonder if we could Zoom?" If they meet in person, they'll be wearing masks. Zoom is best because she'll be able to see their faces.

"We can Zoom." She sounds excited now. "Our oldest taught us."

They agree to Zoom in an hour, after Mr. Ghosh is back from the store.

At the agreed upon time, Rebecca finds herself staring into the faces of a middle-aged Indian couple who look like the type of husband and wife who resemble each other more and more with the passage of time. Mrs. Ghosh wears an orange and red translucent scarf over her gray hair. His hair is still black, combed neatly and gel'ed into place. They clasp each other's hands on the table.

"Thank you so much for agreeing to speak with me," Rebecca says. "Has there been any progress on locating Kabir?"

Mrs. Ghosh shakes her head sadly. "No. Nothing."

"Do the police have any theories? Any suspects?"

"There is one. An appliance repairman who came to our

house to fix our oven shortly before our son disappeared. The police found pornography in the man's apartment. Nothing else, though. It doesn't seem like it could be him."

Rebecca makes a note to herself to get his name before they end their Zoom. "Can you tell me about Kabir? His personality. Things he enjoyed doing."

"He is our third and last child. Our baby. No one could be sweeter. I admit we spoiled him."

Mr. Ghosh nods his head in agreement. "He was a quiet child. Shy. And very smart. He received straight A's in school."

"Was he ever in any trouble?" She has to fish to see if there might be a connection to Antoine.

"Oh no," Mrs. Ghosh says. "He always did as we asked him. We almost never had occasion to scold him."

She sees it's going to be difficult to get them to admit their child could've been anything less than perfect. But she perseveres. "Is it possible, though, that he had any friends who might've been a bad influence?"

They exchange a look now. "There was one boy who Kabir knew," Mr. Ghosh says. "The police said the boy was a thief and asked if Kabir may have been involved in that. Of course, our boy would never do such a thing. He was brought up to be honest."

Second note—get name of this boy before hanging up.

"His teachers said so many good things about him. His English teacher thought he was gifted."

Gifted. Didn't Ethan's teacher say the same thing about him? Was this villain only interested in gifted boys? It might be worthwhile to talk with this teacher, who could be more forthcoming than Ethan's. "What was his English teacher's name?"

"His name?" Mr. Ghosh looks confused. "I don't remember."

"Mr. Flannery," Mrs. Ghosh says. "He isn't at our local school any longer. I believe he took another job."

It hits Rebecca like an ice-cold hand reaching into her chest and squeezing her heart. *Mr. Flannery.* Ethan's teacher. It can't be a coincidence. It can't be.

Mr. and Mrs. Ghosh are looking at her curiously. She struggles to pull herself together. "Do you remember his first name?" Her throat feels scratchy.

Again, an exchanged look, then Mrs. Ghosh shakes her head. "Is it important?"

"I don't know," she manages to say. "He might have noticed something in the classroom."

"Of course," Mrs. Ghosh says. "Would you like to come to our house? We are not worried about Covid. Maybe you would like to see Kabir's room?"

Rebecca feels like weeping for them. She knows so well how they feel. How desperate they are for someone to take an interest. Anyone who might give them hope their son has not been forgotten, abandoned, and presumed dead.

"This is all I need for the moment," she says. "I promise I'll let you know personally if I learn anything that might be useful. Thank you so much for speaking with me."

Mr. Ghosh bows his head, while his wife clutches his arm and presses her forehead against his shoulder. "We appreciate the call," he says.

It's only after the Zoom has ended that Rebecca shoots out of her chair. *Mr. Flannery.* She can't remember his first name either, so she checks the school website. *Todd Flannery.* She finds a short bio that lists Kabir's local school as the place he worked previously. *It must be him.*

When she thinks about it, she remembers feeling a little odd at the time that Mr. Flannery was the only person she'd spoken to who offered an alibi. An alibi she never bothered to check. She isn't much of a detective when it comes down to it. He said he was away camping or something the weekend Ethan disappeared. He easily could've been lying. But it would be hard to verify one way or the other if he said he went alone.

He's a school teacher. He isn't a despicable old Fagin-esque character who pimps out child thieves. He's not an asshole who cheats on his wife with his hairdresser and then hides that information instead of helping to find a missing child. He's either honest and reliable, or he's hiding something that's infinitely worse than marital infidelity. If Ethan went to see him that night… the fact that Todd Flannery never came forward to say so is damning.

She texts Ian once more, apologizing for the short notice. *Can you get me Todd Flannery's home address?* She explains he's an English teacher at Ethan's school.

Ian's reply comes a few minutes later. He's getting information for her faster and faster; she can tell he's getting caught up in the case as well. She checks his message, and cold certainty rushes over her. Flannery lives in the town where Ballard dropped Ethan off.

It's him. She feels it in her bones. She's aware she's told herself that before. But this time… this time, she has to be right. She checks the time—eleven fifteen. He should be at school for the next few hours at least. Is it all remote learning now? The kids for sure, but maybe not the teachers. They have all their resources in the classroom. She doesn't think they teach from home.

To be sure, she calls the school and confirms that Mr.

Flannery is in his classroom. He lives about forty-five minutes away. It ought to be enough time for her to search the place before he leaves school for the day.

It would be safer to wait and do this in a mindcast. On the other hand, if Ethan is being held prisoner by his teacher, she can only save him by going there in real-time. If he's even alive to be saved.

She throws on sturdy boots and a jacket. At the last minute, she grabs a hammer from her toolbox and sticks it in her bag. It ought to break a window with no problem. What if she's wrong, though? Or what if there's no evidence? She could land in jail herself.

Past the point of caring, she rushes out to her car.

Chapter Forty-Five

HER DRIVING IS erratic and Rebecca prays she doesn't get pulled over by a traffic cop. She breathes in deeply, trying to calm herself. For what she has to do next, she must be cool-headed.

Rows of trees on both sides add privacy to Flannery's house, which huddles at the end of a cul-de-sac. She parks along the curb across the street before crossing to his neat lawn and following a quick path to his front door. No one answers her ring after several tries. Unsurprisingly, a check of the knob finds it unyielding.

She steps back from the door to survey the place. No signs warn of a dog or an alarm system, nor do any cameras appear to be pointed at her. A front window that she could reach and break with her hammer can be viewed by neighbors across the street.

She hurries over the lawn to a wooden side gate. This too is locked. However, it isn't terribly tall, and it has no pokey things on the top. Making sure there are no witnesses behind her, she drops her bag on the other side. Her hope is to pull herself up and neatly vault over the gate. Needless to say, this takes way more effort than expected, but she finally manages to haul herself clumsily to the top, before falling on the other side. At least she lands on her rear.

In the back of the house, with no windows within easy reach, it appears she'll have to go all out for the sliding glass door. She checks it first in case he forgot to lock it. No such luck.

It occurs to her she ought to muffle the sound of the hammer, but she hasn't brought anything for that. Except she does have on a light hoodie over her shirt. She whips this off, wraps it around the hammer, and takes a wide, two-handed swing, imagining Flannery's smarmy face instead of the window. It cracks nicely, and she pounds it twice more until she has a clear reach inside to the latch.

Just as she steps gingerly over the broken glass, the ring of her phone makes her start. She should've shut that thing off. She silences the ringer inside her purse without checking who's calling. No time for distractions now; she needs to be quick.

She makes a rapid pass through three small bedrooms upstairs, two of them used for storage. Maybe later she'll have to search inside the boxes, but that will only happen if there's nothing larger and far more obvious to be found.

The place is neat and clean enough, though the scent of cigar smoke clings to its walls. Downstairs there's a kitchen and a separate small dining area, a living room and den, a bathroom, and laundry room. Except for the drab color scheme—fifty shades of brown—and the lack of decoration, the house could not be more normal. What if she's wrong and Flannery has nothing to do with these disappearances? Maybe it's only a coincidence that he taught both boys. She doesn't actually know if Ethan came here. Maybe he planned to visit his teacher but then changed his mind after getting dropped off. Some random sicko prowling the streets might've snatched him. She should've thought of that.

But she's here now and needs to make sure she's covered every inch of this place. The kitchen is the last room she enters, and that's where she finds the door to the basement.

Basements are not common in California homes. The presence of one makes her wonder if Flannery had this home built for himself. Or if he searched far and wide before finding it.

The light bulb at the top of the steps works, thank goodness. The stairs seem strong enough, certainly not like they'll break under her weight. She retrieves the hammer after removing the hoodie that's now embedded with slivers of glass and sticks it back in her bag. That and her phone might be needed in the cellar, though she doubts she can count on a signal down there.

Despite trying to reassure herself there's probably nothing but dusty old comic books and logs for the fireplace to be found, her throat goes dry as she begins her descent. At the bottom, she discovers the furnace, a set of faded wooden cabinets, and a mini-fridge that isn't plugged in. Before looking through them, she continues around the back of the stairs, where there's a door.

It's locked, of course. She prays this doesn't mean she'll have to search the entire house for the key. If it were her, she'd keep it out of sight in the basement. She switches on her phone flashlight to begin her search, determined to check for spiders before putting her hand into any dark crannies. She looks above the door frame, behind the furnace, and underneath the stairs. Nothing. She opens the mini-fridge to find a quart of milk on the shelf. *Ew.* She's about to move on to the cabinets—which she's dreading—when it strikes her that no smell arose from the fridge. It isn't plugged in; the milk ought to have curdled.

She grabs the carton and sniffs. Definitely no odor, and it's so light, it's probably empty. She sprays her light inside it. *Ha!* The key is here. She shakes it out onto her palm and unlocks the door with trembling hands. This is the moment of truth. If there's nothing here but garden tools, she'll have to start over. She won't give up, though. Not ever.

The door creaks as she pushes it inward. And there it is. She enters the room in a state of stunned disbelief.

Ethan is not here now, thank god. Not him nor any other child. But there can be no doubt regarding the purpose of this room. A flat table with shackles forms the centerpiece. He must've restrained the boys here. On the wall there's a selection of knives straight out of a medieval torture chamber. That's what this place is, she realizes. A torture chamber.

A shudder sweeps through her whole body. She thought she was prepared for the worst, but not this, she could never have imagined this. She clutches her arms around herself to still the shaking. *Ethan.* How he must have suffered. She turns to flee out of the room and back up the stairs, but Flannery forms a dark silhouette, standing in the doorway with a gun.

Ethan

Chapter Forty-Six

ETHAN LOSES his appetite after Antoine sends the threatening text. Thoughts race through his head. Maybe it's not as bad as he thought. He could leave home for a while and let things blow over. If enough time passes, the old man might forget about him.

He needs money to tide him over for a few months. That should be enough time. After that, he can come back home. If he doesn't go to the police—and he won't—Antoine will hopefully leave him alone.

Uncle Ray told him San Diego was nice. It's warmer there, summer is coming, and he can sleep on the street with other homeless people. Just for the summer, then he'll come home.

He'll write to Ma when he gets there, so she won't worry. Aunt Yakeera will help her. She'll take her in; she has enough room, since it won't be Ethan too. By the end of the summer, Ma should be recovered and can get a new job. When Ethan comes back, they can find a new apartment, a smaller one they can afford. It would be best if they move to another town, where Antoine can't find him. But none of this can happen till Ma gets better.

His mind races, putting together the plan. He goes to his room and gathers the small amount of cash he has. He glances around at the stuff he owns, wondering if any of it is worth selling. Sadly, he doesn't think so. Then he changes into his newest jeans and sneakers. Grabs his warmest jacket. He pockets the burner phone Antoine gave him, hesitating a minute, wondering if Antoine can track him from it, then scoffing at himself for such a stupid idea. Antoine isn't the police or the FBI. He's just a broken-down old son of a bitch.

While Ethan's getting ready, he's thinking about what to do first. Aunt Yakeera will give him some money if he asks, but he can't tell her what he's about to do. No way would she allow it. She'll tell Ma and they'll maybe call the police to find him and bring him back. She might even force the truth about Antoine out of him, which could be dangerous for all of them.

He needs a story, and he thinks he may have one that will work.

Before leaving, he checks on Ma. She's dozing, as she so often does these days. From the half-empty vodka bottle by her bed, it's clear she's been drinking again. Maybe that means the nausea caused by the concussion has gone away, but he can't rejoice over that if it just means she's going to return to the booze. He tiptoes over to her and brushes his lips against her forehead. *Love you, Ma,* he mouths.

He checks out the window for any sign of Antoine on foot or in his car. Since the coast looks clear, he heads out and sets a rapid pace for Aunt Yakeera's house. Her car is in the driveway so he figures she's home, but when she doesn't answer his knock right away, he lets himself in with his own key. He's about to call out when he notices movement on the couch. His aunt and a man he's never seen before. They're kissing and... *shit.* He immediately regrets coming here, wishes he could unsee what he just saw. Turning back, he stumbles out the front door.

"Ethan!" Aunt Yakeera calls out.

He actually pauses on her front lawn, not because she called him but because he doesn't know what to do now; he had been counting on her. While he's trying to figure things out, she hurries up to him.

"Ethan, you didn't see that. He's just a friend of mine, but... don't tell your Ma or anyone else, okay? Why'd you come over? Is everything all right?"

"Yeah... no. Wanted to talk to you, that's all."

"We'll talk, honey. My friend is leaving. Let me take you somewhere. Your favorite restaurant, okay? You wait in the car. I'll be right out."

Not knowing what else to do, he sits in her car and waits. A few minutes later she returns and gets into the driver's seat. The stranger is still in her house.

Chapter Forty-Seven

AFTER A FEW MINUTES of sullen silence in Aunt Yakeera's car, Ethan abruptly opens up the subject he'd come to talk to her about. "Can I borrow some money?"

She glances sideways at him. "I've been helping out your mother. Does she need more?"

"Not her, me."

"You can ask her for it."

"I can't tell her about this. She can't handle it right now." He wonders if he looks as frightened and upset as he feels.

"Can't handle what?"

"I borrowed money for a new phone. I've paid back some of it, but there's a lot left. The guy who loaned it to me says if I can't pay it now, I have to sell drugs for him."

"Who is he?"

"Can't tell you that."

"Tell the police."

"Can't do that either. You know how it is."

"Boy, what kind of people have you got yourself mixed up

with?" She almost doesn't brake in time to avoid hitting the car in front of her. "How much money do you need?"

"Two hundred bucks."

"If I give you this, you have to promise not to have anything to do with this guy again."

"Promise. I didn't know he was part of a gang."

"You also have to promise if he keeps bothering you, you come to me and tell me who he is then. Okay?"

"I promise. If he won't leave me alone, I'll tell you."

"You ought to have a phone, that's for sure. We'll stop at the ATM," she says. "There's one on our way."

Later when they're seated in the restaurant, she hands over the cash. "Remember what I said."

"I know. Thanks."

Their drinks arrive shortly after they place their orders. "Glad I got this," Aunt Yakeera says, sipping her margarita. "What a day. Honey, the man who was at my house… just pretend you never saw him, okay? He's married, and if his wife finds out, he'll be in a lot of trouble. You're old enough to know how that is."

Sometimes Aunt Yakeera forgets he's really not that old. How would he know how it is for a married man to cheat on his wife? "Why you wanna be with a married man?" Ethan says. His aunt is not that old, and she still looks nice. There ought to be plenty of unmarried men she could date.

"It's complicated. At first I didn't know about his wife. Anyway, after tonight… I don't think I'm going to see him anymore."

Ethan is anxious to get to a different subject. "I'm worried about Ma."

Yakeera focuses on him. "I know, honey. But she's going to get better, I'm sure of it."

"I guess so. But I worry cuz, you know, if something happened to me, who's gonna take care of her?"

"What are you talking about? *Nothing* is going to happen to you. And anyhow, as soon as she gets well, she'll be taking care of *you*, not the other way around."

"I know, but it might take a long time for her to get better. And you know, shit happens all the time around here. A two-year-old kid got shot three days ago. So I just wanna be sure, if something happens to me, you'll take care of Ma."

"Nothing's going to happen to you. But yeah, I'll always be there for my sister. You don't give up on family, not ever."

"You'll make sure she's okay?"

"Course I will. So will you. Because you'll be right here watching out for her alongside me."

He takes this as sufficient promise. The food clatters down in front of them, and he eats fast, hunger overwhelming him. At the same time, he makes a decision. He can't go back with Aunt Yakeera. Antoine might be hanging around the neighborhood looking for him. He can't take the chance of his aunt seeing him or learning anything about him.

When he's taken his last bite, and she's still barely midway into her meal, he excuses himself to go to the bathroom. He glances back to confirm she's not looking before ducking out the front door of the restaurant.

Chapter Forty-Eight

HE'S CROSSING the parking lot, about to check his phone for the nearest bus stop where he can catch a ride to the central terminal, when a car coming from the lot pulls up beside him. The window slides down, and the driver leans sideways to speak to him. "Hey, you're Ethan, right?"

Ethan recognizes him as Aunt Yakeera's boyfriend. *What the fuck is he doing here?* "Uh, yeah," he says, still walking.

"I'm John. I realize that must've been weird for you back at the house. Sorry. Can I give you a lift somewhere?"

John, huh? He could've been more creative with his fake name. But Ethan is poised between curiosity and thinking the wise thing would be to run like the devil out of here. Curiosity wins, mainly because he really does need a ride. Normally he would do anything rather than get into a car with some strange dude who might be a serial killer for all he knows. But with all that's happened in the last few weeks—Ma's accident, Antoine's threats, Teshi going into a coma—he's developing a real *what the fuck* attitude. Whatever he does, right or wrong, shit is happening, so he might as well pick what's convenient and worry about the rest later.

So he gets into the car with the white dude whose name probably isn't John, and they drive off.

"Where are you going?" John says.

Ethan doesn't want him to know his destination is the main bus terminal because he might tell Aunt Yakeera later on. Instead, he asks him to drop him at an intersection near there.

"Your aunt's real nice." The dude's smile looks like a leer to Ethan. This is a conversation he definitely doesn't want to be having. He turns to stare out the side window.

"But I'd appreciate if you don't tell anyone about me and her," John continues.

Ethan is about to tell him he doesn't give a single fuck about him or his sordid affair with Aunt Yakeera, but a sudden thought stops him.

"Sure," he says. "I won't say a thing." He pauses like the next subject isn't related. "Did you know my ma lost her job? And then she got hit by a car?"

"Oh wow. I hope she's all right."

"Not really. She's dizzy and confused all the time, so she can't work right now. We can't pay the rent. I think we're going to get evicted." Ethan gives the man his most tragic expression.

John gets it. "I can help this one time."

They drive a few blocks and stop at an ATM. When he comes back, he hands over a pile of bills.

"I got you a thousand," John says.

Ethan can't believe his eyes. He sure made the right choice to ditch his aunt at the restaurant. On the other hand, this dude is clearly bribing him to keep his mouth shut.

There's so much worst shit happening, he can't worry about that now. With this money, he and Ma can afford to pay next month's rent. He can't run away now. But he still has the problem of Antoine. He needs help, or at least advice. He glances sideways at his aunt's boyfriend, thinking white people hold more sway with the police. Maybe John could make a deal for him—turn in Antoine and they don't charge him with anything.

But then, this is a guy who cheats on his wife, bribes kids, and probably lied about his name. He can't be trusted to help Ethan. He doesn't want anyone to know he has anything to do with Ethan's family. All he wants is to keep his secret.

But Ethan knows another white dude who he actually trusts. Mr. Flannery. Maybe his teacher can help him. Maybe Mr. Flannery can find him a smart, free lawyer who can get him out of this mess. He should go talk to him. Maybe not tell him what he did. Say that he's asking for a friend. In fact, he can use Teshi. It's already known that Teshi was caught stealing. He can say, he wants to help Teshi once she gets out of the coma.

He turns to John. "I changed my mind about where I'm going." He gives John the address of the lady who fired him as a dog-walker. He can ask her which house belongs to Mr. Flannery.

His teacher will help him. He's sure of it.

Chapter Forty-Nine

IT TAKES some time to get to Mr. Flannery's neighborhood, but John doesn't complain. Nor does he seem at all interested. He will do what Ethan wants this one night, as long as he never hears from him again and as long as Ethan does not talk about what he saw at Aunt Yakeera's house. That's how it seems, at any rate.

John does not appear at all concerned about letting Ethan out in this dark neighborhood with no one around. As soon as the boy shuts the door, he swerves into a tight U-turn and speeds away.

Unfortunately, the dog lady's house is completely dark. He checks the time—only a little after nine. Could she be in bed already? She might be furious if Ethan wakes her up.

He decides to walk down the street and check out the other houses. Maybe he'll glimpse his teacher through a window. If that doesn't work, he'll check Google to see if he can dig up Mr. Flannery's address somehow.

The suburbs, so unlike his own neighborhood, make him uneasy. Sure, where he lives, there are lots of sketch people hanging on the street, all day, all night. But there's some security in knowing people are around. Here, it's just like, dead. There are street lamps, but the houses are mostly dark. It's incredibly quiet; not even any dogs barking. Probably sleeping inside with their owners. It's so eerie, it makes him think of a sci-fi story where all the humans have been kidnapped by aliens.

He's beginning to wonder if he should've come here. He probably would give up on this idea right now, except it's a long walk from here to the train. Everyone he saw when he went on the practice dog-walk was white, and Ma has warned him about wandering in such places, especially after dark. Police get called when folks see you passing through, and then it's shoot first, ask questions later.

But he gets lucky when he reaches the house at the end— a plain gray home with narrow green trees on both sides that look like rows of soldiers. A barren hill looms behind the place. Most importantly, an old-fashioned dark blue Chrysler is parked in the driveway. Mr. Flannery's car.

He's relieved to see lights on in the house. He wonders if he should search for his teacher's phone number to give the man a heads up before Ethan arrives at his door. But Ethan knows he's just trying to delay the inevitable. Better to be bold, march right up, and press the doorbell with confidence. His teacher might be annoyed to see him at first, but he'll understand once Ethan tells him what's going on.

He does pause before ringing, though. Wondering for the first time if Mr. Flannery is married or has anyone else living with him, he listens for voices. But it's silent inside, without even the sound of a TV show. That seems incredibly strange to Ethan. At this time of night, the TV is always on in his apartment. Maybe it means his teacher is already asleep and just forgot to turn the lights out. He tries to peer in through the windows, but the blinds have been lowered on the first floor.

Fuck it. What's the worst his teacher can do? Ethan rings the bell, and listens for the sound of movement inside, but it's just as quiet as before. He waits, though. He's committed now.

Two minutes later, still no one has come. He rings a second time. All remains quiet inside. He waits a little longer before deciding to leave. But just as he starts to turn away, he hears something. Footsteps, definitely. Approaching the door. A pause while Mr. Flannery is probably checking the peephole. Ethan makes sure to stand in full view of it, to reassure his teacher it's only one of his students.

The door comes open. Ethan thought Mr. Flannery would look surprised or angry, but instead he stands there with the same inscrutable expression he displays every day in the classroom. He wears what must be a relaxing at home outfit—a light blue long-sleeved t-shirt, faded jeans, and slippers. Ethan doesn't think he's ever seen him wear jeans. The weirdest thing is seeing his teacher holding a cigar that looks like it was lit right before the door came open. Ethan had guessed already that Mr. Flannery liked them, but it's one thing to guess, and another to see proof.

"Come in, Ethan." His tone is relaxed, just as if he had been expecting him to show up.

"Sorry to bother you at home," Ethan says, even though Mr. Flannery doesn't seem bothered. He follows his teacher into the living room.

"I hope your mother knows you're here." He gestures at an armchair for Ethan.

The boy sits. "No one knows I'm here. I came to ask you for advice. For a friend."

"You walked from the train?"

"Yeah." Ethan's not sure why he lies about it. Maybe because he sensed Mr. Flannery wanted that answer.

"Did Ms. Paladino tell you where I live?" he asks.

Ethan shakes his head. "I saw your car."

His teacher settles into a hard-backed chair next to the table, sucks in a puff of cigar smoke, and blows it toward the door. He pulls a crystal ashtray closer to himself and pats the cigar over it.

"Which friend needs advice?" he says.

Now that he's with Mr. Flannery, Ethan is feeling more and more nervous about explaining the problem without implicating himself. He rubs his leather band, looking around the room. The wall paint is white, the carpets are light brown. The furniture is mostly brown too. There are no pictures on the walls. It's as if Mr. Flannery doesn't want visitors to know anything about him.

"Teshi." There's no harm in naming her, since everyone already knows she's a thief.

Mr. Flannery looks puzzled. "I didn't realize the two of you were friends."

"We met when we were little kids."

"She isn't like you. She's made terrible choices with her life."

"I know that, but I want to help her. She's in a coma, you know." He forgets Mr. Flannery was the one to tell the class.

"I'm aware. Of course, we all hope the best for her. But it happened when she trespassed on someone's property and tried to steal from them. Such actions have consequences."

"Well, before that happened, she told me something

about her situation. There's an older man who's like sixty that Teshi was working for. This guy's a real villain. Anyway, once she stole something for him, the man threatened her. Told her she had to keep doing it, or he'd turn her in. He had evidence, you know. Pictures. So Teshi was stuck. She had to keep stealing for this dude, like, forever. And I'm wondering, if she comes out of the coma, do you have any advice for her? How she can break away from his control?"

"Ethan, if she comes out of that coma she's going to be arrested. That's what she needs to be worried about. The criminal will disappear from her life. Teshi won't be any use to him anymore."

Unfortunately, Ethan's not ready with a counter-argument to this. "Well still, I mean, if something like this happens to someone else... what do you think they should do?"

Mr. Flannery's lips form a grim line. "Are we sure we're talking about Teshi here?"

Ethan moves his trembling hand out of sight under his thigh.

"Are you in trouble, Ethan?"

Mr. Flannery's tone frightens him. He lowers his eyes from his teacher's penetrating stare. This is when he notices the line of red on the edge of Mr. Flannery's sleeve. It looks like blood, though there's no wound that Ethan can see.

When he lifts his gaze to his teacher again, Mr. Flannery is staring at him with wide eyes magnified by his glasses. Ethan feels as if his teacher is seeing right into his mind and reading his thoughts. He shivers.

"You've disappointed me." Mr. Flannery's voice turns frigid. "I thought you were one of the special ones. Different. I believed you had it in you to break out of your toxic environment. Clearly, I was mistaken. You're stealing now, is that it?"

Ethan lowers his head. "I stole a few things. But I don't want to do it anymore. I made a mistake. But now it's like… this dude keeps threatening me."

"I wish you had thought of that before you started."

Emotion swells inside him and he's dangerously close to bursting into tears. "Can I use your bathroom?" he asks in a quiet voice.

Mr. Flannery glares down at him while he inhales from his cigar. He breathes out the smoke slowly, watching the shapes it forms as it drifts upward. "Down the hall," he finally says, with a nod in that direction.

Ethan follows the corridor to the bathroom. He has to go badly; the soda he drank at the restaurant has caught up with him. But while he stands there peeing into the toilet, his gaze wanders to the bathtub next to him. The rust-colored shower curtain is pulled shut. But near the wall, on the exposed edge of the beige tub, Ethan sees a thin streak of dark red.

At the same time, he becomes aware of an odor that's like what he has noticed before in the butcher department of their local supermarket. An odor he couldn't smell in the living room, with the cigar smoke overpowering all other scents.

The hair rises on the back of his neck as he finishes peeing and zips his pants. Like someone in a daze, he reaches to the curtain and draws it open. The shower rings screech against the metal bar, but he can't stop himself from looking now.

A motionless gray cat is splayed out on its back in the center of the tub. A horrible gash runs the length of its belly, covered in a sickening spray of darkened blood. At first Ethan thinks it's fake, someone's demented idea of a Halloween prank. But then he realizes it's real, and it's dead.

With all his nerves tingling in dread, he backs away from the disgusting sight. Mr. Flannery must've done this. Mr. Flannery, who Ethan believed was a moral, upstanding, responsible adult who he could count on for advice. Mr. Flannery, who tortures cats.

Ethan's instincts, heightened by recent events, kick-start his self-preservation mode. He turns and flings the door open. Runs out into the hall, ready to bolt from this house of horrors into the street, and take his chances running all the way to the train.

But Mr. Flannery is at the end of the corridor holding a gun. "It's a shame you had to see that, Ethan."

Rebecca

Chapter Fifty

"DROP your purse and back away from the door." Flannery keeps the gun trained on her. "I don't know who you are, only that you'll regret breaking into my house."

Since she's not an expert in firearms—or anything else—she doesn't know what kind of gun it is, or whether it's even loaded. She can only assume it has the potential to kill her instantly, and therefore, she lowers the bag that holds the hammer along with her wallet, keys, and phone, and steps backward.

"Lie down on the table," he says.

Her gaze shifts to the torture table and her heart sinks.

"If you don't, I'll just shoot you right now. If you do, who knows, maybe you'll find a way to escape." He gives a dry laugh at the apparent absurdity of that notion.

Still, it's the exact reason she lies down on the table.

"Attach the leg cuffs around your ankles." He waits while she places both leather restraints around her ankles and buckles them.

"Now do your right hand with your left."

It's difficult since she's right-handed, but she manages it.

He approaches and sets the gun on the workbench. "Stay absolutely still. Otherwise, I'll take one of those knives and get to work on you. Also, just a heads up, the room is sound-proofed so there's no point in screaming."

With only one hand still unrestrained, she knows there isn't any way she can disable him or free herself. She has no choice but to allow him to buckle the leather band around her right wrist. She's completely at his mercy now.

He opens her bag on the table, gets out her personal items, and shuts off her phone. "I assume that's your car across the street."

She says nothing. She's done making things easy for him.

He flips through the wallet, which doesn't have a whole lot in it. "Rebecca," he reads her name from her driver's license. "Why are you here?"

"I work for the police. Undercover. If you let me go immediately, things will go better for you."

"It's funny you don't have a badge. Or a partner, apparently. So I ask you again, why are you here?"

"I'm investigating the disappearance of Ethan Pitt."

He flinches at this. "Ethan. The boy who fell from grace."

"You kidnapped him and held him here."

Flannery gets a far-away look in his eyes. "He came here of his own free will. I tried to resist. At first I didn't answer the door, but he wouldn't go away. Even when I let him in, I wasn't planning to keep him here. But once he confessed his crimes, I knew what had to be done."

What little hope she had now drains from her. He would not be telling her this unless he planned to kill her.

"I cared for the boy," he continues. "He needed release from his earthly form, before the corruption grew so deep, there would be no chance of redemption. To keep my resolve from weakening, I allowed him to find the cat I had released earlier that evening."

"Cat?"

"Animals have a life force too. During release, their essence flows through me and brings me closer to divinity."

It's official, then. Flannery is completely insane. "I don't understand. Did you torture the poor thing?"

He screws up his eyes at her. "Torture? No. My methods are humane. I drug them. I don't want them to feel pain. That wouldn't do at all."

It gives her some relief to hear that Ethan didn't suffer.

"We start out life pure and uncorrupted," he says. "Some few manage to remain that way. Most fall prey to evil influences; by the time they reach adulthood, they're beyond help. But the children whose stars shine the brightest... if and when their light starts to dim, there's still time to save their souls."

"You seem to think you're doing them a favor by killing them."

"Even you might gain something from it." He takes a bottle out of a drawer. *That's it.* He's going to drug her, and then... her gaze shifts to the knives. "My team knows I'm here," she says. "They'll be coming any second." He gives her a look like he doesn't believe her. She's never been a convincing liar.

He brings a glass of water from the small sink and shakes out she's-not-sure-how-many-pills into his palm.

"Don't do this! I can help you. They're going to catch you anyway. If you haven't hurt me, they'll go easy on you."

He lowers the glass near her head and grasps her jaw, pushing her mouth open. Just like when Antoine forced the alcohol into her, Flannery drops the pills in the back of her throat. She tries to block them with her tongue and spit them out, but he prevents her. He pours water into her mouth, while she gags, unable to keep herself from swallowing. The pills go down.

"Bastard." Her eyes fill with tears. This isn't what she expected to happen. Why was she so foolish to have done this alone?

He returns the bottle and glass to their places. "It's going to take a little while to have an effect." From this, Rebecca figures he's given her sleeping pills, or something similar. Most likely he wants her alive when he cuts into her with those knives.

He puts her things back into her bag and takes it with him when he leaves the room. The snap of the lock from the other side saps the last tendril of hope from inside her heart.

Chapter Fifty-One

COURAGE AND DETERMINATION. Not so long ago, she assured herself these were her special skills. *Use them, dammit. Don't give up. Never admit defeat.*

She looks down at her right wrist and wonders how she can possibly get free. Her hand faces up, and the back of the leather restraint is attached to a short metal chain, which is screwed to the table and probably bolted on the other side for all she knows.

The good news is she would not need a key to undo the restraint, which is buckled like a belt. The bad news is she can't do it without a free hand, or at least a way of rubbing her wrist against something. There isn't enough chain to allow her to turn her hand and move it against the table or even against her own body.

Without being able to reach over with her other hand, or swivel her wrist to press against the table, there appears to be no way to get the cuff off. Still, without expecting anything, she strains to pull her hand up. If the chain isn't securely attached, maybe she can break loose.

But it is secure, and pulling on it only makes her arm ache. Then she tries her left side, and both of her legs. She's not sure, but she thinks the left wrist might be slightly looser than the right. Turning her head sideways, she's able to glimpse the chain that's attached to the table. It looks old, even a bit rusty. This prompts a shudder at the thought of how many times it might've been used over a period of many years.

She yanks at the left chain again. Definitely looser than the other side. She thinks she sees a slight gap in one of the links. Maybe if she pulls hard enough, she can open it sufficiently to break the connection. One more time, and now she uses all the force of her left arm to resist the chain. Her muscles are screaming, and the edge of the cuff is digging into her flesh, but she won't let herself stop. *C'mon. C'mon.* She twists her body away to apply more force.

The link snaps free and a feeling of elation fills her. But it's short-lived; there's still much to be done. Flannery could return any second and he has the gun.

It's awkward and way too slow undoing her right hand, but she manages it. Sitting up to release her ankles, a wave of dizziness hits her. The drug is starting to do its damage. Her throat feels dry, but she can't let herself think about it. She frees her ankles before sliding off the table, nearly falling in the process. Her balance is off.

She's going to need a weapon, and there are plenty of them, though she recoils from the thought of stabbing anyone with a knife. Nevertheless, she's like Goldilocks, picking out the one that fits her hand the best. The one that has the right weight and size for her to use comfortably. She tiptoes to the door, trying to be as silent as possible, since she has no idea how close he might be.

The door is locked, of course. He would not be foolish enough to leave it unlocked, even with her restrained on the table. Her gaze sweeps the room, wondering if there might be a key in here. She seriously doubts it, though, and it might rob her off whatever wakefulness she has remaining if she were to search for it.

She'll have to wait for his return. She positions herself behind the door because there's no other hiding place. But while she crouches there, her symptoms grow worse. She feels nauseous and her head is starting to throb. It's a struggle to keep her eyes open.

She thinks she might've dozed off by the time she hears the key in the lock. Her eyelids refuse to raise more than half-way. She jabs her fingernails hard into her palms to keep herself awake a little longer.

The door comes open. She can't wait to see if he's holding the gun or not, she has to act. Driven by a rush of adrenaline, she whirls around the door and meets his shocked expression with a thrust of the knife into his side. He cries out and sprawls to the floor, blood gushing out.

It isn't in her to plunge the knife in again and again, as she probably should do to save herself. She draws it out and flings it across the room so she'll have her hands free, to somehow get around him and through the door. Her only thought now is to flee.

But just as she thinks she's gotten past him, he grabs her ankle, catching her in mid-stride. She crashes hard onto her knees. Turning back, she sees his hand reaching into his pocket where the gun must be. With her free leg, she kicks his wound with every bit of strength she has remaining. He screams, releasing her, and she scrabbles across the floor to the stairs on the other side, too dizzy to stand up.

Using the banister, she drags herself up each step. When she's almost to the top, a shot rings out. She feels nothing and hopes that means he missed her. Sheer terror gives her the jolt she needs to conquer the last onslaught of stairs, and stumble toward the table in the kitchen, away from the doorway.

There are noises behind her. A banging against the stairs. He's not dead, he's forcing himself up them. Probably pulling himself just as she did. Determined to kill her. Determined not to let her leave this house alive.

She's fading fast. Any second now, she'll be passed out and helpless. Grabbing the leg of the kitchen table, she struggles to pull herself up. But the table wobbles and a heavy crystal ashtray falls from it, landing on the other side. She falls back down and reverts to crawling. Halfway into the hall, her body collapses. This is it, she can't get up, can't move a single muscle any longer. She looks back to see him reaching the landing, blood smeared all over him. He raises himself to his knees to take aim at her. He's going to kill her.

But his hand trembles, his body sways. He's trying to steady himself before taking his shot. In the second this gives her, one final surge of energy allows her to lunge for the ashtray. In the same movement, she rolls up and hurls the heavy object at Flannery.

It hits his forehead. He staggers and falls backward down the steps.

She drops to the floor again, unable to keep her eyes open a second longer. As she lies there, strange visions flash inside her head. Her body shakes uncontrollably. She's not sure how much time has passed when she feels the touch of a hand on her back.

Ethan

Chapter Fifty-Two

UNDER NORMAL CIRCUMSTANCES, Ethan would probably have frozen at the sight of a gun. But after everything he's been through—the stealing and the threats and Ma's accident and Teshi's coma—he almost doesn't care if Mr. Flannery shoots him. Almost. At least, he's reached the point where he'd rather be shot than captured.

These thoughts take a fraction of a second to ignite inside him, and then he's moving. He charges Mr. Flannery, taking him by surprise, knocking his right arm hard against the door frame. Mr. Flannery drops the gun, howling in pain. With no time to grab it, Ethan kicks the weapon away as he flies out of the room, sprinting faster than he ever has in his life, across the main living area and out the front door.

"Ethan, you fucking get back here!" Mr. Flannery bellows.

But he's on fire now. Bounding through the streets, he almost wishes someone would see him and call the police. He sprints all the way to the train station, though he fears Mr.

Flannery may have driven here already and be lying in wait for him. He slows as he approaches, checking the parked cars, and the shadows for anyone lurking. So far, no sign of his teacher. Mr. Flannery may be too weak to do much now because of his injured arm. Or he might be afraid cameras would catch his movements.

Ethan has a bit of luck, finally. The last train of the night arrives within minutes of his reaching the platform. He gets in, keeping his eyes on the window, watching in case Mr. Flannery appears at the last minute and boards the train too. But soon enough the doors close and his teacher hasn't come.

Still, he remains nervous and walks through the train until reaching a section where several alert-looking riders are seated, as opposed to the two passed out homeless guys in the first car he entered. If Mr. Flannery appears out of nowhere and tries to kill him, at least there will be witnesses.

On the way, he makes his decision. When he reaches his stop, he no longer runs, but speed-walks to the homeless camp. He wanders for several minutes before spotting Uncle Ray's tent in a new location. Ethan kneels by the opening, listening to his uncle's light snoring.

"Uncle Ray," he hisses.

No response.

"Uncle Ray," he says louder.

There's a snort and then, "Who is it?"

"It's me. Ethan."

"What you…? Get in here, boy."

He climbs into the tent as his uncle pulls himself into a sitting position. "You alright?" he says.

At that moment it hits him how definitely, positively not all right he is. His eyes fill with tears and the story of his life these last few weeks pours out of him, except he leaves out the part about Mr. Flannery, afraid that his uncle might do something rash. When he finally finishes, Uncle Ray leans forward and wraps his arms around him.

"What am I going to do, Uncle Ray? What am I going to do?"

"'Run like hell my dear,'" his uncle says softly, "'from anyone likely to put a sharp knife into the sacred, tender vision of your beautiful heart.' A brilliant poet named Hafez said that."

He nods at his uncle. "Will you come with me?" he asks.

THEY LEAVE before dawn and take the train into San Francisco. Uncle Ray gives Ethan his tent and helps him settle into a camp. He tells the boy not to go anywhere aside from fetching food occasionally.

Uncle Ray returns to his camp on the other side of the bay for several weeks, as long as it takes to convince police he has nothing to do with Ethan's disappearance.

Then he returns to his nephew in San Francisco, and together they take the bus to San Diego. Ethan feels guilty for not reporting Mr. Flannery to the police, but he's certain they're not going to believe his word over that of his respected teacher. Especially if Antoine spreads it around that he's a thief, and then he'll be the one going to jail. It's a terrible thing if Mr. Flannery continues to cut up cats or other animals, but after all, Ethan is just a kid and can't be expected to solve the world's problems himself.

He pretends to be Uncle Ray's son as they build a life together. He takes a new name for himself. *Amari.*

From time to time, he thinks about calling his mother. But he's afraid she won't be able to keep it to herself that he's still alive. And if word gets around, Antoine might threaten her to force Ethan back under his control. For now, it's better if they all think he's dead.

Rebecca

Chapter Fifty-Three

2020 - PRESENT

REBECCA WAKES up in a hospital bed with Sadie seated beside her. She squeezes her sister's hand.

"They pumped your stomach." Sadie says. "You could've died."

"I know," she says. "What about Flannery? Is he dead?"

She shakes her head. "They took him off to jail hospital or something. They found the stuff in the basement. Jesus, Becca, how many kids are you planning to save?"

"All of them. I need to work faster."

"Just as I thought. I didn't tell Dad, by the way."

"Thanks." When Rebecca asked her to be her emergency contact, she made her promise not to tell their father if anything happened, unless death was imminent. "How did I get here? Did the neighbors call the police?"

"Oh no. A man called Ian Slate. Nice name. Do you know him?"

Rebecca smiles. Over the next hour, she tells Sadie as much about the case as she can without mentioning time travel. Hopefully Sadie will assume any confusing parts are a result of her sister not being quite clear in the head yet. Rebecca isn't ready to reveal her mindcasting superpower to anyone, not even Sadie. Her sister might question her sanity, or leak it to their father, who would definitely question her sanity. Maybe she'll confide in them eventually. But not today.

By afternoon, Rebecca is able to check out and return home. The first thing she does when she's alone is arrange a Zoom with Ian.

"How are you feeling?" he says.

"Not bad. Thank you. I'd be dead if not for you. How did you know where I was?"

"I'd be a lousy private eye if I couldn't guess that. I've observed you; you're impulsive. The last thing you did was ask for Flannery's address, and after that you stopped answering my calls. I did some research of my own and learned he was also Kabir Ghosh's teacher. Then I drove to his house, and just as I was tracing the plate of a nearby car to see if it was yours, I heard a gunshot."

"Oh man, that was lucky," she says.

"Lucky it didn't give me a heart attack. I called the police, and then I went in through the back like you apparently did because I wasn't sure they'd arrive in time. But there wasn't much I could do till the ambulance arrived."

"He wasn't moving around, I hope."

"He looked dead. So did you. This was very traumatic for me. Do you think you could give me a heads-up next time?"

"Seems like a typical day for a hard-boiled detective like you," she says.

"I told you, my typical day is following women to hotels and hanging out in the lobby, trying to snag free lemonade while I'm waiting."

"Do you even play the violin?"

He gives her an enigmatic smile before signing off, leaving Rebecca feeling like she'd be happy to actually hang out with him instead of only ever seeing him on her computer, but… Covid. In-person meetings will have to wait.

A FEW DAYS after Rebecca returned home, she heard from the police that the bodies of three juveniles were found buried in Flannery's back yard. So far. The news hit her hard, and for the next day she found herself weeping on and off at unexpected moments. She had really believed she might find Ethan alive.

His family was notified that he might be one of the victims, due to Flannery having been his teacher. DNA results had not come in. Rebecca had not yet spoken to them, nor to Kabir Ghosh's parents.

She did not regret any of her actions. As the sister of a kidnap victim, she knows it's better to learn their fate than to spend your life wondering if they might still be alive and suffering in the den of a monster.

The police questioned her regarding her role in exposing Flannery. She managed to gloss over the information she learned through time travel by describing it as conjecture. Her choice of journalist as a cover turned out to be a good one, as they accepted her refusal to divulge the names of "witnesses" who spoke to her. That Ian was known and respected by some of the officers helped her credibility.

On the fourth day after Flannery was exposed, she's getting ready to call Yakeera. But Yakeera calls her first.

"Rebecca?" Her voice is filled with a joyous excitement Rebecca doesn't understand.

"He's alive," Yakeera says.

Rebecca's breath catches in her throat. "What?"

"Ethan. Ethan is alive. We just spoke to him on the phone." It all comes spilling out in one rapturous run-on statement. "The night he disappeared, that devil Flannery tried to kill him or take him prisoner, I don't know which, but our boy got away. His uncle Ray helped him. He loves Ethan, always did. Ray hid him, and then they went to San Diego together, and they've been doing well. They got a tiny apartment somewhere, and it's not bad. Ray got a steady job in construction and bought a used car. Ethan's doing remote school. And can you believe it, he's taking care of dogs for six different families.

"Ethan didn't actually know his teacher was murdering kids; he thought it was just cat torture, which is bad enough, but I don't blame the boy for running, there was so much going on back then, way more than a thirteen-year-old could handle.

"Anyhow, Ethan saw the news about Flannery getting arrested and bodies turning up in the backyard, and he knew what we would be thinking so he called us. Rebecca, he's grown so much, so mature, he wants to testify against Flannery and another lowlife called Antoine. He was so, so happy to hear Teshi came out of the coma. He's dying to see her too.

"I'm calling to let you know he and Ray are driving up here and will arrive around noon today. Laila and I thought you might want to be here. You made this happen, Rebecca. It's thanks to you our boy's coming home to us."

Tears of joy stream down Rebecca's cheeks. "Thank you, Yakeera. It means a lot to hear you say that."

As soon as they hang up, Rebecca leaps out of her chair, shrieks, and does a happy dance. She calls Ian next and probably sounds a lot like Yakeera just did in relaying the information.

Arriving early for the reunion, she parks across the street, trying to peer in through the windows to check if Ethan has come yet or not, but the glare makes it impossible. After waiting in her Honda for about fifteen minutes, she decides Ethan probably is inside and she should go to the door. But just as she grabs her purse, a car approaches, slows, and parks on the other side.

She recognizes Ray in the driver's seat. He remains there while Ethan pops out the other side. It gives her a shot of euphoria to see him, looking completely different than when she spoke with him during the mindcast. Then he was gaunt with bent shoulders and a vacant stare. He's alive again now, approaching the house with bouncing steps and a wide grin spread across his face.

Laila flings the door open and rushes out first, wrapping her arms tightly around her only child, who she hasn't hugged for over a year. Yakeera gives them no more than two seconds before she flies out and joins the embrace, hopping up and down for joy.

Arms still clasped around one another, they squeeze into the house, with one of them kicking the door shut behind them.

All the effort, all the fear, and all the pain were worth it for this. Rebecca starts her car and drives away. This is a moment when four would be a crowd. Ray gets it too.

Chapter Fifty-Four

2020 - PRESENT

AT THE END of the week, Rebecca decides to go to dinner at her father's house after all. They greet her warmly when she arrives, even Marie. Rebecca is beginning to believe she hasn't given her stepmother a fair shake. Or her father.

She and Sadie assemble Legos with the boys while her father and Marie prepare the meal. At dinner they talk about Covid, of course, but also about politics and philosophy and art and math and lots of silly subjects too. When Marie goes off with the boys to help get them ready for bed, the three remaining adults dispatch the kitchen cleanup quickly.

They play Pictionary after the boys have gone to sleep, and it's the most fun Rebecca has had in a long time. But scribbling on pieces of paper reminds her of the suicide note her mother wrote and makes her heart harden against her father again.

Maybe it's the wine they had with dinner, or maybe it comes from observing Ethan's courage in returning home and facing his demons… but after her father finishes using the bathroom, she meets him in the hall to have a private word.

"Can I talk to you, Dad? It's important."

"Sure, Rebecca." He leads her into the small room he calls his study.

"Something has been weighing on my mind," she starts right in. "Something that came out in therapy." She's not even in therapy right now, but he doesn't know this. "I remembered that when we found Mom, there was a piece of paper on the table next to her. You took it away and never showed it to me. Was it a note? Did she leave us a note?"

He looks at her blankly before getting up and leaving the room. She hears his footsteps on the stairs.

She's not sure what she's supposed to do. Did she upset him with her question? Does he want her to go now? Her father can be infuriatingly uncommunicative at times. But just as she is resigning herself to leaving without any resolution, she hears his steps returning.

He has a folded piece of paper in his hand. "It was in the safe in our bedroom," he explains. "I'm so sorry, Rebecca. I should've given it to you years ago. In all honesty, I forgot about it. Or more accurately, I pushed every memory of that day as far from my mind as possible."

"But why didn't you let me see it then?"

"You were so young. I guess I was thinking, we could pretend it was an accident. Not that I ever thought for a minute that it was. But… I wanted you to think that. It's such a terrible thing to believe someone you love could've killed themselves. You feel responsible. Though it isn't anyone's fault, you can feel a crushing guilt. I blamed myself. I still blame myself in some ways.

"But it was wrong of me to hold this back from you once

you were an adult. In fact, it was written for you, not me." He holds it out to her.

She hesitates before taking it. For better or worse, she must read it.

THE NOTE SAYS: "Dearest Rebecca, I wish I could've been the mother you deserve. Forgive me." While her father waits, she reads it over and over again, its words washing over her. *Dearest. Forgive me.*

Nothing will ever cure Rebecca of the guilt and remorse she feels as a result of her mother's suicide. But the note brings relief. Her mother isn't blaming her for anything. Quite the opposite. She recognizes her own incapacity to mother after having lost one child. It isn't that she didn't love Rebecca. It's that she felt herself deeply inadequate.

She's not sure how much time passes before she rises and lets her father take her in his comforting embrace. She doesn't cry; those tears have been shed before. Instead, she feels like she can breathe again.

"I love you, my darling girl," he whispers. When they break apart, she discovers he's the one whose cheeks are damp. He wipes his face before they rejoin the others.

Before leaving, Rebecca hugs Sadie and Marie, and then holds Marie's hands while thanking her warmly for the dinner. She hasn't been fair to her and it's time to change all that.

Sadie and Marie clearly know something happened in the study, but they are wise enough not to ask about it now. She will share the note with Sadie the next time the two of them are alone together. Now is not the time. The note was for Rebecca. She needs to savor it for a while.

At home, she learns from the news that Kabir Ghosh has been confirmed as one of Flannery's victims. She calls his parents immediately to express her condolences, but no one answers. Their grief, like Laila and Yakeera's joy, is not to be shared, at least not yet.

She prepares herself for bed, hoping the closure will at least allow her to get a decent night's sleep at last. But when she settles under the covers, her thoughts go to the night she shared drinks with Lou inside The Blazing Horse pub. It's the one remaining mystery of this entire adventure. What happened to him? Where is he now? Why did he leave the school where he had just begun teaching?

It's clear he cares about the welfare of children. She wonders if that means he's wounded like her. She felt a connection to him that night.

The curiosity is killing her. She closes her eyes and pictures that night in the pub. Before long, her head heats up, her vision blanks out, and she spins backward through time on her way to solve the mystery of Lou.

Amari

Chapter Fifty-Five

AS AMARI STARES *out at the ship that is now a tiny blip on the horizon, he remembers the words of the village Wise Man: "Do not confuse futile pursuits with those actions that are within your power to accomplish."*

His gaze shifts to the waves crashing on the rocks below, but he no longer considers dashing himself against them. He climbs back down from the cliff and heads in the direction of the largest village along the coast.

At first, he is reviled as a beggar and a thief, because word has reached them from the other villages. But he humbles himself, and is satisfied to earn pennies from the washing of villagers' feet. He sleeps along the side of the road like a dog until a family takes pity on him and invites him to share their home. They do not regret it, because not only is he kind and honest, but he is also hardworking and helps every member of the family with their chores.

As he grows older, his skill as a storyteller begins to emerge and he earns his keep that way. Eventually he becomes so accomplished at weaving his stories that he is elevated to be the new village Wise Man, as the previous one unfortunately passed away. At eighteen years of age, he is the youngest Wise Man the village has ever seen.

He could, if he wishes, live out his life in this place that has welcomed him and made him one of their own. He could find a bride and with her, make a family of children. He will be prosperous and respected and live a happy life.

But one day word comes of a group of like-minded people in a faraway country called England, who have gathered to condemn the practice of slavery. They mean to fight those who think they have the right to rob the health, happiness, and freedom of others.

Amari knows much he could tell them about this practice. He can bear witness to the crimes against his family and the people of his village, wrenched from their homes, and forced into slavery in a foreign land.

Thus he finds himself, six years after the cruel act that tore his world apart, on a ship headed for England. He leans into the wind at the bow, leaving behind the home he worked so hard to construct. But someone must stand tall against the brutality of evildoers if they are to be stopped.

THE END

Please read on for a sample of *Dreadmarrow, The Thieves of Magic Book One.*

CHAPTER ONE - TESSA

TODAY, my fifth time as a russet sparrow, I felt as if I'd been flying all my life. I left caution behind, soaring over the town square, catching a beakful of rancid smoke rising from the shops and ramshackle homes. My wings flapped according to instinct and carried me toward Sorrenwood's outer edge, over rows of broken shelters. I continued across a field dotted with bent farmhands, past a thicket of trees that gave way to the swimming hole.

I flew lower to watch the three bare-chested boys who approached the water. I'd seen them before but they were younger than me and I could not remember their names. The dark one swung out on the rope and when he reached the highest point, he released with a shout and a splash. His friends followed in rapid succession, nearly landing on him. Their joy was infectious. I sailed up higher and dove down, letting myself fall until—an inch above the water's surface—I pulled up. The pale boy saw me and looked puzzled. He had probably never seen a bird play before.

I rose higher for my second dive. But as I shifted downward, a huge silhouette appeared above me... *a hawk,* its wings spread wide, a monstrous beast to sparrow-me. Shaking, I dodged left and then right and then back again, hoping to confuse it with my odd movements. I followed an erratic course and didn't realize until it was too late, that I'd crossed over the outer wall and now flew above the Cursed Wood. Gray mist seeped upwards like steam from a giant cauldron. The tips of black tangled branches reached toward me, but I knew better than to land on any of its foul trees.

The air whooshed as the hawk dove for me, and I felt a stinging sensation as it clipped off a wad of my feathers. I beat my wings in a panic, angling toward Fellstone Castle. It was a dreary, forbidding fortress but the only place I might find refuge. A shadow formed over me as the hawk prepared to dive again. My confidence shaken, I swore at myself for having so little practice flying. Whether to flap my wings or coast on the wind—I had no idea which would get me to the castle quicker. And so I flapped and coasted and flapped again, aiming to reach the nearest tower. The hawk's breath grazed my back as I flew over the moat, ducked under the edge of the roof, and hurled myself into a tight corner, where I crouched, trembling and desperately wondering what defense I could use if my attacker crawled in after me.

The hawk didn't come. Yet I feared it might still be out there, perched on the roof, waiting with uncanny stillness for me to emerge. That didn't sound like normal hawk behavior, but I knew so little about them. By now I should've been an expert on any animal that wished to make me its supper. I'd grown careless, caught up in the novelty and excitement of flying. My first time out, I only hopped across the yard and took a short flight up into the nearest tree, growing accustomed to the odd sensation of seeing things behind me. With each day I flew, I grew bolder. I'd half-believed, half-hoped the magic lent me a kind of protective shield, keeping other animals from perceiving me. I knew better now. In future, I would watch for shadows, and feel for subtle shifts in the air that flowed around me.

Movement below caught my eye. Down on the castle lawn, six armed boarmen huddled together, speaking amongst themselves in snorts and grunts. Their pig heads with sharpened tusks were disturbing enough at the best of times, combined with the bodies of herculean men, broadened by thick padding covered in chain mail. Here, alone and unprotected at the castle, I shivered in dread, and shrank further into my corner. Their leader glanced upwards, revealing heavy scars across his eyes and snout. Even from this distance, or maybe because I knew the way they always looked at you, I felt the chill of his cold, black piggish eyes, devoid of feeling. Of course he wasn't looking at me, a little bird under the roof, but at an open window below me. Seconds later, a man extended his arm out the window and lowered it in signal.

The scarred boarman bellowed at another whose ear had been partly chewed off. The group opened up, revealing a frail man on his knees at their center, his hands tied behind his back. Pale and filthy with his clothing torn into strips, he looked as if they'd dragged him from the dungeon only moments earlier. Two of the boarmen lifted him to his feet and shoved him in the direction of the forest. His poor legs appeared weak and spindly from long disuse, but still he loped toward the trees, driven by a final, desperate hope that defied all logic. *If only I could help him.* But even if I flew down to lend him my wings, by the time I changed back, and before

I could show the man what to do, the boarmen would surely have murdered us both.

Run, I silently urged. *Run as if the world were on fire beneath your feet.*

The boarmen salivated and raised their spears on their leader's command. The man stumbled just before reaching the trees, clawing his way up, fighting his way forward. *Faster! Don't give up!* The leader signaled for the boarmen to unleash their blood lust, and they pummeled each other to be first to their prey. They thundered across the field, hunched over and pig-like despite having the bodies of men. Their high-pitched squeals formed a grating war cry as they crashed through the bramble into the woods. Seconds later came a heartrending shriek that froze my blood. The trees shook during the killing frenzy that must have followed.

I couldn't bear to watch any longer. I set out from my refuge, meaning to fly directly home, but instead, curiosity drew me to the window below. I had to see with my own eyes the devil who had ordered that brutal execution. Landing on the sill in the corner, I told myself there was no danger because I looked like nothing but a harmless little bird. At worst he might swish me away, and I would fly off before his hand could touch me.

The man was Lord Fellstone himself. Stripped to the waist, he sprawled in a chair by the window, his feet propped on a low table, and his hands overloaded with jeweled rings. He looked as he had when I last saw him at the Midsummer celebration, with a mane of auburn hair that, considering his age, ought to be showing some grey. His nose was sharp, his eyes shrewd, his manner bored.

But it was the tall young woman beside him who drew my eye with her extraordinary appearance. She was dressed like a man, in close-fitting apparel sewn of dark green leather. She wore a cloth cowl of the same color round her head and neck, hiding her hair. A thin leather mask covered her forehead, cheeks, and the top of her nose, leaving open her mouth and chin. This woman hunched over Lord Fellstone, holding a sturdy, intricately carved wand of black wood. Its tip caught a beam of sunlight from the window and diffused it into a wide circle over a pustulent boil on Lord Fellstone's shoulder. The infection gradually cleared until it was gone. She moved the wand over a second boil that sprawled in a circle of virulent red near his waist.

His lordship raised his head and gave me such a piercing look, it caused the contents of my stomach to flip. His eyes widened in astonishment, until a loud, "Ha!" burst from him.

The woman paused. "My lord?" She followed his gaze to sparrow-me. I tried to leap into the air and fly away, but somehow I couldn't get my claws to let go of the sill. I didn't know if I was frozen in panic or rooted in place by a silent spell Lord Fellstone cast on me.

"Oh, I do love sparrows," he said. He leaned forward, his face growing animated. "You know, this one would make a splendid appetizer for my supper tonight."

"Boiled or roasted?" said the woman.

"Cooked over an open flame on a skewer, I should say. Fetch me my sword."

I couldn't believe my ears. No sensible person would ever eat a sparrow. For two tiny bites of stringy meat, it would not be worth all the trouble of plucking. *Is his lordship mad?* I strained to pull my feet away, while they stubbornly clung to the sill.

The woman lay down the wand and retrieved a sword with jewels encrusted on its handle.

"There won't be anything left of it after we spear it with that," Lord Fellstone said, making me wonder if he'd been playing with me all along. "Why is this bird still here anyway?" His lips curled into a smile that was ripe with evil intent.

My claws released and I shot up into the sky. I raced across the Cursed Wood and over the castle wall with one goal driving me: *get home.* Once during the flight, a shadow moved over me, but it was only a crow. As I reached the house and swooped down toward my window, the crow circled above and turned back the way we'd come. *Did the bird follow me?* I dismissed the thought as quickly as it occurred. My nerves were frayed; soon I'd be imagining eyes peering out of every tree.

The instant I touched my bedroom floor, I scraped three times with my claw. The familiar tingling sensation shot through me as I changed back into myself, Tessa Skye, sixteen years old, wearing a plain wool gown that laced up the front over my white shift. My key pouch hung from a belt that cinched my waist. It was odd how anything I wore or held onto when I changed into a bird would still be with me when I changed back, but magic was a powerful force beyond my understanding, and sometimes one had to simply accept what was, without being able to explain it.

I remained frozen for a moment, struck by the memory of that terrible hunt on the castle grounds. The shrill cry of the wretched man echoed still inside my head.

"Tessa."

I jumped and spun around at the sound of Papa's voice. He stood just behind me, framed by the doorway.

"Papa?" I said, giving him a blank look, masking my fear of what he might have seen.

His form seemed more gaunt than usual, his features stern and angular, his cheeks darkened with the stubble of three days' growth. His eyes fixed on the sparrow amulet that hung from my neck. Normally I tucked it out of sight under my gown, but I hadn't had time.

"Where did you get that?" he said.

I felt my face flush red, but I rallied, affecting a light tone. "I thought you'd gone out."

"The windrider," he said. "Tell me where it came from."

"The what?"

"Your amulet."

I hesitated before answering. "I found it."

"Where?"

"I don't recall."

"Don't tell me a falsehood. I know it was your mother's."

I wanted to bolt but he filled the doorway and I would never make it past him. "I remember now. She gave it to me," I said.

"No, she didn't," he said.

"How do you know?" A tinge of defiance crept into my voice.

"You were only four when she went away."

The old feelings of hurt and abandon rose. "I suppose she didn't love me enough to give me anything."

Papa scowled. "Don't talk nonsense. Tell me the truth. How did you get it?"

"I found it on her bedroom floor, the day she left," I said at last. "Was it so awful to take something that reminded me of her?"

"It's not a memento, it's a rare item of powerful magic. Give it to me."

I shrank back from him and clutched my throat. "No, Papa!" He had no idea what he was asking.

"You heard me. Magic is dangerous. Only the conjurers are allowed to use it. If it were up to me, it would be banished altogether."

"But you don't know… you've never felt… there's nothing else like it. Flying is pure and it makes me feel free, and…. How could anything be wrong with it?"

"You can be sure there's a price to be paid in using that magic. Not knowing what that price is makes it all the more troubling." He reached out his hand. "You're young yet. Be patient and good things will come, but not this way."

My eyes filled with tears as I lifted the necklace over my head and handed it to Papa. "I meant no harm."

He softened at the sight of my tears and clasped me to him. "Of course not. You didn't know the danger. Now you do. We'll speak no more of it." He held me for a moment. "Have you been to the Kettlemore's yet? We can't afford to scorn paid work."

I forced my gaze from the hand that clutched my sparrow. "Yes, Papa."

He had called it a windrider. The name suited my amulet; I would use it from now on. I would not despair of flying again, as I had my ways of bending Papa to my will over time. He simply didn't understand and I must find a way to convince him of the benefits. Perhaps he could be made to grasp its value by trying it himself. He would not want to, of course. And the truth was… I didn't want to let him use it. *It's mine and I should not have to share it.*

End of preview.
Please visit margiebenedict.com for purchase options.

Acknowledgments

My deepest love and gratitude goes to these dear friends and voracious readers for their willingness to read and honestly critique all that I write:
Karla Sheridan
Katherine Liscomb
Sheri Davenport
Susan Rendina
Tanner Kaptanoglu

Thank you to the many readers who have lent their support to indie authors like me. By showing your appreciation of my work, you motivate me to continue this writing journey.

Margie Benedict writes emotionally resonant, genre-defying fiction rooted in the power of second chances. From coastal suspense to time-twisted mysteries and sweeping speculative worlds, her stories follow characters who rise, reclaim their agency, and rewrite their destinies.

Formerly publishing as Marjory Kaptanoglu, Margie is an award-winning author praised by Kirkus, Publishers Weekly, and the BookLife Prize. Her work blends gripping tension with deep emotional stakes, drawing comparisons to *The Time Traveler's Wife*, *Outlander*, and the twist-driven novels of Lisa Jewell.

Before turning to fiction full-time, she developed pioneering software at Apple Computer and wrote screenplays that were recognized by the Nicholl Fellowships and produced for film.

Margie is now building a brand readers can trust for gripping, transformative storytelling—books that don't just entertain but empower. From middle grade fantasy to adult thrillers, sci-fi, and women's fiction, she invites readers of all ages to ask: *What would you do with a second chance?*